D1559219

PICKED COTTON

Cotton Joe's throat was dry and he cursed himself for being suckered that way by an Indian and a kid. Now he was going to lose his gun and the money he had in his pants pocket; he was going to say goodbye to two saddle bags crammed with supplies and likely his horse as well. He pictured Jake's face when he'd finally trudged back to the camp and explained how he'd lost his mount.

"Get down!" said Cuchillo.

"Down!" echoed Marty and vaulted to the ground.

Joe did as he was told, careful not to give either of them an excuse to shoot. If he was going to get robbed there wasn't much point in stopping a couple of slugs in the process.

It was only when they tied him to the nearest tree and the Apache produced the knife from behind his back that Cotton Joe slowly began to understand that it wasn't his horse and money they were after at all.

The Apache Series:

ATTENTION: SCHOOLS AND CORPORATIONS

PINNACLE Books are available at quantity discounts with bulk purchases for educational, business or special promotional use. For further details, please write to: SPECIAL SALES MANAGER, Pinnacle Books, Inc., 1430 Broadway, New York, NY 10018.

WRITE FOR OUR FREE CATALOG

If there is a Pinnacle Book you want—and you cannot find it locally—it is available from us simply by sending the title and price plus 75¢ to cover mailing and handling costs to:

Pinnacle Books, Inc.
Reader Service Department
1430 Broadway
New York, NY 10018

Please allow 6 weeks for delivery.

_____Check here if you want to receive our catalog regularly.

APACHE
#24
DEATH RIDE
William M. James

PINNACLE BOOKS   (◎)   NEW YORK

This is a work of fiction. All the characters and events portrayed in this book are fictional, and any resemblance to real people or incidents is purely coincidental.

APACHE #24: DEATH RIDE

Copyright © 1983 by William M. James

All rights reserved, including the right to reproduce this book or portions thereof in any form.

An original Pinnacle Books edition, published for the first time anywhere.

First printing, March 1983

ISBN: 523-41675-X

Cover illustration by Bruce Minney

Printed in the United States of America

PINNACLE BOOKS, INC.
1430 Broadway
New York, New York 10018

DEATH RIDE

Chapter One

"Damn fine feller! Damn good man! Injun or no injun, you're white as fer as I'm concerned. You hear that everyone? Fer as Big Mitch Gresley's concerned, this man's good as white."

Gresley swung his paw of a hand through the air and brought it down with a hearty slap high on Cuchillo's back. His round, bearded face was flushed with drink and excitement and his breath stank of bad whiskey.

Cuchillo stood his ground, hoping Gresley would wear himself out and then he could quit the trading post and get on his way. Gresley had hired him a couple of months back to ride out into the desert and bring back a wagon load of supplies that had got stranded out there when the driver had been attacked and left for dead. As things went, the driver had been alive—just—and he'd made his way to the nearest settlement and told his story before he pegged out.

Now Cuchillo had done what that man had failed to do and wasn't Big Mitch making good and sure that everyone knew!

"Damned if you ain't white under that skin, feller. Good as white!"

Cuchillo didn't rightly take to the idea of being good as white. Most of the whites he'd ever come across had been a long way from what Cuchillo would have called good. He'd met two white men in his life that he trusted: Hedges, who had been his teacher, and Lovick, the pony soldier.

Cuchillo shuddered. He couldn't stop himself thinking about the white man he'd hated above all others. The image forced itself into his brain like bitter phlegm rising from the back of his throat. Cyrus Pinner who had killed his wife and child and mutilated his right hand.

Pinner was a white man!

Cuchillo was not white!

He shrugged Gresley clear with a sudden movement of his powerful shoulders and strode towards the door, men stepping out of his path.

"Hey! Hey, feller, what the hell you doin' there?"

Cuchillo carried on going.

"You ain't ridin' out, are you?"

It seemed that he was.

"Don't you want your money or nothin?!"

Cuchillo's left hand stilled on the handle of the thick oak door. Of course, he wanted his money. He spun back around towards the bearded man and was on him as fast as he'd moved away.

"Money," said Cuchillo, his hand stretched towards Gresley.

"Hey, now! Take it easy! You ain't got no call to go stompin' off like that. Not when I'm telling these men here what a good injun you are. Hell, feller! You ought to be pleased some of these folk are even lettin' you drink in here. Knowin' what your kind is like when they gets too much liquor inside 'em."

Cuchillo's face darkened in a scowl.

Big Mitch wasn't quite that drunk he couldn't read danger in the Apache's face. He clapped him on the arm and assured him he didn't mean nothing by what he said; he asked Cuchillo to have another drink with him to prove it

But Cuchillo had already drunk enough whiskey to blur his mind a little and he didn't want it to get any worse. Not tonight. The post was packed with perhaps forty men, all of them pretty deep in liquor, and if any trouble was to bust out, he didn't fancy his chances any too good.

"Thanks, no. You give me money. I will ride. Ride now. Okay?"

Mitch Gresley blustered and fumed some, but in the end he agreed and he went—none too steadily—over to where his saddle bags were hanging from a peg at the side of the room.

Cuchillo waited, head high, aware that from time to time men in the post were looking at him, making remarks that he couldn't hear.

Maybe that was just as well.

Gresley slapped a bundle of bills down into his hand. "There you go. That's what we reckoned, an' I've put in another ten dollars on account of you doin' the job so quick. How's that?"

"Good," nodded Cuchillo. "Thanks."

"S'okay," Gresley slapped the Apache's shoulder again and laughed, "takes an honest man to 'preciate another. That's what I always say."

"Maybe we do business again," said Cuchillo, stepping back.

"You betcha, feller. You an' me, we can do business any time." He pointed at where Cuchillo was pushing the money down into the back of his pants. "Ain't you even goin' to count it?"

Cuchillo shook his head. "What you say about honest men. That is true, no need to count."

Big Mitch Gresley shook his head slow. "I'll be damned."

Cuchillo nodded once more and turned for the door. Outside he was struck by the cold clearness of the night, the absence of tobacco smoke and liquor fumes. Out here his own mouth tasted foul, his being somehow sullied by the men he had been with. For him it was too often like this—caught on the rim between his own world and that of the conquering white man.

Cuchillo looked at the whiteness of the moon and his voice was soft and smooth as steel. "Cuchillo says, he who hunts with the coyote and the vulture, carries the stink of death with him all his days."

The moon stared back down at him blankly. No one else heard or answered. Back inside the trading post someone had struck up a tune on a squeezebox and there was the sound of stomping feet and clapping hands.

Cuchillo moved quickly to where he had tethered his horse. He would ride out of hearing from the trading post and make camp. It was a good night for sleeping with the stars. Then in the morning he would head north. There was a town less than half a day's ride off where he could buy food and maybe find work. But with good money in his pocket, there was no longer any urgency for that.

There was a smile on the Apache's face as he pulled himself on to the back of the bay gelding and touched his heels to the animal's sides. As man and animal cantered away, the night wind stung their faces and a night bird signalled their coming.

In a small clearing between some pines, Cuchillo hobbled the gelding and stretched out his blanket. He collected wood and built a small fire to keep the worst of the cold from his bones. Had he had any of the white man's coffee, he would have brewed some before sleeping, but there was none. Tomorrow, when he reached the town.

Cuchillo lay on his back and looked at the formations of stars spread above him. When his eyes closed, he feared that he was going to dream of his wife and child and he turned in upon himself and tried to send them from his mind. The only way he could live at peace with their loss was by not picturing them as they were when they were alive. To think of their life was to think of their death:

to think of their death was to recall the manner of their dying. To do that was to be filled with such loss and hatred that the only thing Cuchillo wanted to do was to plunge his knife into his enemy until it was buried to the hilt in blood.

And when he felt like that, his enemy was the ancient one: it was the white man.

If the white-eyes had not come to the land with their cattle and their gold and their whiskey, with their railroads and their guns, then Cuchillo would still have been living with his people. He, the grandson of the great Mangas Colorado, would have been one of the chiefs of the Mimbrenos Apache and his wife and child would have been alive and honored—his son would have been growing into his own rightful place in the line.

Instead. . . .

Cuchillo pressed his head down against the earth and forced such thoughts out. He thought instead of the story his grandmother had told him about the trickster and as he did so a smile gradually came to his gaunt face. And with it, sleep.

Amigo reckoned itself a real friendly town. There was a board leaning over against the

south road that announced a population of
two hundred and forty-seven. Beneath that
in red lettering was the warning:

No Chinks!
No Niggers!
Stay out or Else!

You couldn't get a deal friendlier than
that—it didn't say a damn thing about Indians. Cuchillo fought a grim smile back into
place and grunted at the gelding; he'd ridden
this far north to pick up some supplies and
get himself some ammunition for the Colt
.45 that was rolled inside the blanket behind
him. As it was, that seemed the best place
for it. Some white folk didn't take any too
kindly to an Apache coming into town with
a gun sticking up out of his belt and they
were likely to get an itchy trigger finger before they asked any questions. Ordinarily,
Cuchillo might not have found that too threatening a prospect but since he didn't have a
single cartridge left for the .45, it was about
as inviting as stepping into a bull ring with a
red shirt on and all the walls too high to
jump over.

Cuchillo cleared his throat and spat.

There were only a few folk on the dusty
street and none of them seemed to give him

more than a second glance. That suited him
fine. He looked at the stores and the saloons
and picked out a place with a sign hanging
over the short stretch of boardwalk—

Mercy Gladwin: Mercantile and Trading
Dry Goods and Firearms, Ammunition.

A black and white mongrel stirred itself
enough to leave off biting in its coat for fleas
and chase across the street, yapping at the
heels of the Apache's horse. A couple of
back kicks from the gelding gave it other
ideas and it limped back into the shade to
lick itself and indulge in a little self-pity.

Cuchillo looped the reins about the hitching post and waited while a white-haired old
man came out through the store door, favoring a shrivelled right leg.

He stared at Cuchillo like he'd suddenly
come face to face with some scabrous ver-
min. Cuchillo didn't as much as flinch—in a
white man's world he was used to being
looked at like that. If he reacted every time
some fool stared at him that way, he'd take a
day and a half to get along the main street of
every town on the frontier.

The white-haired old timer limped away
and Cuchillo stepped inside the store and
pushed the door to at his back. A small iron

bell above the door rang discordantly to an-
nounce the arrival of a new customer.

Mercy Gladwin bustled out from behind a
brace of flour sacks, rubbing her hands down
the front of her blue and white gingham apron.
She was a taller woman than most. Broader,
too, with a rear end that didn't need a bustle
and breasts that jutted out in front of her like
the proud prow of a boat. Her dark hair was
pinned on top of her head like some kind of
bread wound in thick plaits. She had spiky
gray eyes and a wide, thin-lipped mouth and
when she saw the nature of her customer,
the mouth opened and the eyes narrowed
until they were like tiny gray stones in the
center of her head.

Cuchillo looked back at her and stood his
ground. "I want flour an' bacon, coffee and
some jerky."

"I don't. . . ."

"And some .45 shells."

"I don't. . . ."

"You don't have any?"

"No, I don't serve. . . ."

"You don't serve no chinks an' no niggers.
Sure. I read sign outside town. It doesn't say
anything about Indian. Does not say you will
not welcome the Apache to your town. Sell
him what he want. See! Here! I have money.
White man's money. I pay!"

Cuchillo whipped out the bills from his pants and flourished them in the woman's face.

"See! My money is good. You have what I want, you get it ready for me. Now!"

Mercy Gladwin tried to keep her composure but she wasn't doing too good a job at it right then. Her hands flustered as she was measuring out the flour in three pound sacks and she spilt it over the floor and down one side of her leg. She knocked a box of biscuits over as she reached for the beef jerky. When she was grinding down the coffee beans they kept getting caught in the works of the grinder and the whole thing came to a standstill more times than she could recall happening in a whole week.

Cuchillo sat on a molasses barrel and enjoyed her discomfort.

No other customers came in to disturb them.

It was just him and forty-eight year old Mercy Gladwin, whose life had been dedicated to hard work and bible study and the proposition that if anything gave you more than a twinge of pleasure it was certain to have been brought on to this earth by the devil. That was how she got to feel about the late Herbert Gladwin the night after the marriage ceremony and she didn't change her opinion for the seven years that Herbert struggled along by her side. Finally the effort proved too much for him and he just lay down alongside the trail and died—with a little assistance from a rattler that just happened to have looked up from sunning itself on a nearby rock.

Mercy never missed him—except in the way a dog misses fleas.

Times now, she had to think hard before she could recall his name. He'd never been the kind of man to impress himself on another person and if he hadn't presented Mercy with a way out of Iowa and four hundred dollars, he wouldn't have impressed himself upon her for as long as he did.

Cuchillo, now—well, he was different.

For a start, he was pure-bred Apache and Herbert had been the second generation descendant of an English sailor who'd deserted ship in Boston and married a laundry woman and fathered sixteen children. One of those had been father to Herbert and eleven others and Herbert had been, as you might say, the last of the litter and had always looked like it. Cuchillo looked every inch the son of a great chief.

He was three inches shorter than his famous grandfather and that still made him three inches above six foot. He weighed two hundred and ten pounds and most of that weight seemed to be concentrated in the area of his chest. His legs and arms were strongly muscled and lacked more than a few ounces of fat.

His face was handsome and proud, his eyes dark and set in narrow slits beneath a broad, high brow. He had a nose that was strong as an eagle's beak and which flared out broadly around the nostrils. His bronzed skin was held taut over high cheekbones. His wide mouth was set firm over a firm and resolute jaw. Jet black hair hung down to his shoulders, held in place at the front by a strip of dark red cloth.

He was wearing a white cotton shirt and an old army tunic, a pair of brown cotton pants reinforced inside the thighs.

His feet were sheathed in undecorated hide mocassins.

There was a leather belt around Cuchillo's waist and at the rear of that a sheath which held his knife: *the* knife.

The golden knife from which he took his name.

Cuchillo Oro.

It was a fifteenth century gold dagger with an unusual triangular blade, above which was an ivory handle set in a gold hilt encrusted with precious stones.

Mercy Gladwin could not see the knife but

that did not matter—she was in sufficient awe. What faced her across the bits and chattels of her dry good store was a superb specimen of manhood and one which made her tremble with fear so bad that she could not touch anything without fumbling it over.

"How much?" asked Cuchillo when the storekeeper had finally set his goods together on the counter.

She stared back at him as if he were speaking in a strange tongue.

"How much you want?"

"I ..." She made laborious calculations in her head, using her fingers to help out. "Seven dollars, eighty." she said.

It could have been right or it could have been wrong. Cuchillo only knew it didn't sound too much for what he would be taking. He pulled the money back out from his pocket and counted out nine one dollar bills, waiting while Mercy Gladwin's fingers shook over the twenty cents change.

"Thanks," said Cuchillo, lifting his purchases into his arms.

The woman didn't say a thing. She stared and clung to the edge of the counter and it was clear from her eyes that she still thought Cuchillo was going to attack her and rob the store of whatever plunder he'd set his mind to.

Cuchillo laughed at the woman's fear and pushed open the door out on to the street. He had a couple of gunny sacks tied over the back of the gelding's back, close by his blanket, and he stashed the goods down into these, thinking he'd wait until he was out of town until he used the shells to load up the .45.

He looked up and down the street and where there'd been precious few folk before, right now it was deserted.

He shook his head. The back of his throat was dry like desert sand. He left the gelding tethered where it was and walked diagonally across the street towards the nearest saloon.

The Amigo Palace boasted a pair of batwing doors, one of which was looking decidedly sagging around the hinges. The inside was low and gloomy and most of the tables had their chairs stacked on top of them. One held a mangey-looking ginger cat and another a beer barrel. Not one of them was occupied by a customer.

The barkeep was leaning over the counter that ran down the left side of the room, one eye peering out from under the wide brim of a sombrero. He slowly stood up as Cuchillo walked towards him and it was obvious that he was at least half Mexican. Amigo was a wide-open town after all—not only did they let in Indians, they allowed Mexicans as well. Too bad for the Chinese and the blacks. There were other towns.

The bartender looked out from under his sombrero as if he didn't altogether believe that Cuchillo was there.

"Beer."

The Apache's voice made him start.

"Beer," Cuchillo repeated and set a dollar bill down on the counter.

The Mexican poured him his beer and made his change. It was so quiet you could hear the cat purring from twenty feet away. Cuchillo took the glass over to a table near the center of the room and pulled out a chair, sat down.

There were footsteps outside and he saw someone going past the windows, walking fast. After a while there were a few voices raised and then it fell quiet again. The barkeep had resumed his half-asleep position stretched along the counter.

Cuchillo lifted the glass and swilled the last mouthful of beer around before swallowing it down. He set the glass down with a rap that made the cat move but didn't shift the bartender an inch.

Cuchillo grunted and headed towards the batwing doors.

When he swung one of the doors out and set foot on the boardwalk, the street was still quiet but it sure wasn't empty. There were five men out there, spread from left to right, and every damned one of them was toting a gun and every gun was aiming directly at Cuchillo.

He froze for a couple of seconds, swung his head back towards the saloon. He was in time to see a burly, bald-headed man come through the back door like he wasn't about to take no prisoners. He had a shiny gold star on his leather vest and a shotgun held tight in both hands and the expression on his sweating, mustachioed face made it clear that he'd enjoy nothing more than to blast both barrels plumb into Cuchillo as he stood there.

Chapter Two

Cuchillo held his breath. His weight was balanced on the balls of his feet and he was ready to hurl himself to the ground the second he saw the lawman's finger tighten further across the triggers of the big shotgun.

He watched the hand, watched the face: watched.

The lawman kept coming till there was no more than a dozen feet between them and to unleash both barrels of shot would have certainly meant Cuchillo getting torn apart.

But because he'd got that far without firing, Cuchillo didn't think the man would do it now.

Unless he gave him good cause.

He wasn't about to give him cause.

Cuchillo relaxed onto his heels and slowly brought both arms up along of his head. When

they were high as they could go, and the
fingertips fully extended, the lawman smiled.
There were more gaps in his mouth than
teeth and what teeth there were were mostly
blackened stumps.

"Ken! Howie! Get up here!"

Cuchillo heard running steps and then the
cold steel of a pistol was jammed hard against
his ribs at the left side; a second later the
barrel end of a Smith and Wesson was set to
his temple and in the silence that followed
the triple click of the hammer being thumbed
back was one of the loudest sounds Cuchillo
had ever heard.

"Search him!"

Hands, hard and calloused, ran over the
Apache's body; finally drew the knife from
its sheath.

"Jesus Christ! Will you look at that?"

One of the deputies held the dagger high
in the air and Sheriff Clench whistled and
shook his head and whistled again.

"You reckon this stuff is for real?" asked
the deputy, nodding at the hilt.

"Pends what you mean by real? All that
glitter ain't no gold an' diamonds, you can
bet your life on that. No injun's goin' to carry
stuff like that on him when he can trade it in
for a few bottles of fire-water."

The man holding the gun against Cuchillo's

head laughed and the barrel end vibrated against his temple.

"That there blade that's real. Spanish most like. Seen a few of 'em from time to time. That beauty's real enough to bust you open till tomorrow week."

The deputy snarled and thrust the dagger down into the side of his belt, swinging his pistol back to cover the Apache close.

The sheriff moved closer still, so that the shotgun was staring at Cuchillo like the round, black eyes of a bull.

"That your knife, injun?"

Cuchillo nodded and the big gun rammed hard into his ribs, making his head jerk forward.

"You got a tongue in your head?"

"Yes."

"You understand American when it's spoke at you?"

"Yes."

"Speak it?"

"Yes."

"Then damn well do so."

Cuchillo looked over the shotgun into the round face with its blotches of dried skin and the dark hairs of the sweeping mustache that were fading into gray at the center and the edges. He figured the sheriff for a mighty brave man when he enjoyed those kind of odds. He wondered what he'd be like face to face and without the gun.

"Name?"

"Cuchillo."

"Huh?"

"Cuchillo Oro. It means. . . ."

"I know what it means! Just 'cause you're an ignorant bastard that don't mean everyone else in this country's the same. Gold Knife, it means Gold Knife, right? That fancy pig-sticker you carry round with you that's supposed to impress people, all that fancy fake gold an' all." He moved his head fractionally to one side and spat. "Hell, I know what Cuchillo Oro means okay." He threw back his head and laughed. "An' what it don't mean. An' I'll tell you that—it don't mean shit!"

All three men laughed and again the pistol shook against the side of the Apache's head.

From the noise back of him there had to be quite a little crowd gathering in the street. There was a deal of shouting and none of it friendly—unless you included suggestions for inviting the Apache to a necktie party as friendly. Just a case of Amigo living up to its name.

"Get him down the jail," snarled the sheriff.

The two deputies turned Cuchillo around and started to slow march him along the

street, the sheriff close behind with his shotgun. A couple of dozen townsfolk and a hand-
ful of kids and dogs went running around
them, taunting and threatening all the while.

Sheriff Clench moved on ahead once the
building was in clear sight and used one of a
number of keys hanging from his belt to un-
lock the door. Cuchillo was pushed through
at gun point and made to stand in the middle of the office floor.

A desk had been pushed up against a side
window and it was scattered with papers
and forms and a number of stained cups and
glasses. Over by the back wall a whiskey
bottle stuck its neck up out of a battered
spittoon. There were three straight-backed
chairs, a cot bed by the wall opposite the
desk and a number of fliers tacked here and
there.

Close to the spittoon was the barred door
that led through to the three small and stinking cells.

One of the deputies kicked a chair towards
Cuchillo and the other ordered him to sit
down.

When he was slow about it, he helped him
with a fierce kick in the shins. Cuchillo barely
held himself in check, only too aware the
shotgun was still paying careful attention to
his body.

Cuchillo sat down and looked at the floor.

Sheriff Clench went slowly round behind him and reached forward with his left hand, yanking quick and hard on the Apache's hair. Cuchillo's head came back with a yelp and Clench laughed, spittle flying into the Apache's face.

"What in hell's name d'you think you're doin' here, injun?"

Cuchillo snarled into the lawman's face. Even if he'd had an answer to give he wouldn't have been able to speak.

Clench laughed again and let go of the Apache's hair, so that the head jolted abruptly forward.

Both deputies laughed.

Cuchillo wondered when they were going to start beating him and how far they would try to go. He measured the distance between chair and door, chair and window. The handle of the knife was jutting invitingly from the belt of the one called Howie. Ben was toying with his pistol and letting a sneer sit on his face like a puss-filled boil.

The shotgun was close at his back.

"Why come here to steal?" Clench said suddenly.

Cuchillo's head swung fast. "Steal?"

"Sure. Don't play the innocent with me."

"What did I steal?"

Clench laughed and pointed towards the door. "You got a mount out there with supplies on its back, ain't you?"

"Everything there I paid for. You ask. . . ."

"We don't need to ask. It was Mercy as told us."

Cuchillo sprang to his feet and three guns covered him. Sweat sprang out onto Howie's forehead and Ben's sneer disappeared from his face in a split second.

"She say I steal goods, she lie!"

The Apache was staring direct into the sheriff's face and even allowing for the shotgun, Clench didn't feel any too safe.

"She didn't tell no lie."

"What then?"

The sheriff nodded towards his desk and gestured for Ben to fetch something from its drawers. What he pulled out was a small wad of dollar bills. Clench took them from him and thrust them up into Cuchillo's face.

"Pay for them goods, you say?"

"I pay."

"What with, injun?"

"Money, good money."

"Paper money?"

"Yes, paper money."

The bills were being wafted to an fro before his eyes, tantalizingly.

"This paper money?"

Cuchillo shrugged. How was he supposed to know if it was the same money? It all looked the same to him.

"This money?" Clench persisted. "Was these the bills you paid with?"

"I don't know."

"You don't know!" Clench sneered.

"He don't know," mimicked Howie.

"I bet he don't," said Ben sarcastically.

Clench drew his hand back fast and threw the bills full into the Apache's face. "Payin' with them, injun, that's the same as stealin'. You might just as well've gone in there with a gun an' robbed her blind."

The last dollar bill finished its slow spiral to the ground, landing across the toe of Cuchillo's mocassin.

"Them ain't worth the paper they're printed on!"

Cuchillo looked hard at Clench; he looked at the bills scattered over the floor. He looked at Clench again. It was clear that he didn't understand.

Clench shook his head. "Jesus! You dumb bastard! They're counterfeit, savvy? Some feller with a cheap printin' press run 'em off and he didn't even get the damned picture right! Any one but a five year old kid or an injun would have known they was worthless."

Cuchillo's anger seethed inside. He thought

about all the lies that had sprung from Big Mitch Gresley's mouth like so many poisonous snakes. How he'd gone on about trusting Cuchillo, treating him like a white man! Well, thought Cuchillo, that was right because that was exactly what he'd done—treated him the way the white man always did. He'd cheated him and laughed behind his back and taken him for a drunkard and a fool.

The anger was hard in the muscles of his body and bright in the dark center of his eyes. He would find Gresley. He would teach him a lesson that he would not forget.

But that could only be later. . . .

Now there were three lawmen holding him in a room for a crime that was no fault of his own.

He turned his head left and right, looking from one face to another. He was looking for a sign of compassion, of understanding, of willingness to believe that he was innocent.

Finally he shook his head.

He who looks for water in the desert rock, Cuchillo thought, deserves to die of thirst.

"What you got to say for yourself, injun?" demanded Clench. "What the hell you doin' tryin' to pass them bills here in town?"

Cuchillo shook his head. "I was paid for bringing wagon in from desert. The man who paid me, he give me that money."

"An' you didn't know they was fake?" exclaimed Howie.

Cuchillo shook his head.

"Huh'. Even a dumb injun ain't that dumb!"

Cuchillo turned towards him and raised his fist. It was all the men needed, the gesture they had been waiting for. Clench jabbed forward with the shotgun and the barrel ends struck hard and deep into the rear of the Apache's ribs. He automatically swung back towards the sheriff and Ben lashed at the side of his head with the long barrel of his pistol, missing everything but the ear, the gunsight tearing a gash through the lobe.

Cuchillo roared with anger and Howie aimed a kick at his groin which missed but caught him high in the thigh.

Cuchillo flailed out with his right arm and hit the deputy's outflung leg and sent him staggering back, off-balance.

At just about the same moment, the sheriff brought the shotgun through a high, looping arc that ended at the base of the Apache's skull.

Cuchillo stumbled three paces, grunted, shook his head to clear the blurring of vision.

His knees faltered but held.

The sheriff sent the weapon into another arc and Howie charged at him, head down, aiming for the chest. Cuchillo waited until the deputy was almost upon him and then sidestepped neatly, chopping his stiffened forearm down on the back of Howie's neck as he went past.

Howie went to the floor like a felled ox.

Cuchillo threw up his left arm and blocked a blow from Ben's pistol, which had been whipping towards his face. The gun went high from the deputy's hand and Cuchillo's arm was suddenly cold and numb.

Out of the corner of one eye he saw the fall of the shotgun. He tried to get out from under the swing but he never quite made it. The force of both barrels with Sheriff Clench's considerable strength behind them smacked sickeningly down onto the front of his skull and this time the Apache's legs were like water. His nose struck the floor hard and blood jetted from his nostrils. He rolled over onto one side and boots thudded into him, back and front. He pulled his knees tight into his body and cradled both arms about his head. Kick after kick ploughed into him, Cuchillo keeping his body as relaxed as he could now that his defensive position was assumed. Minute after minute passed in a welter of blows. He could no longer distinguish between them, one boot or another, one aching, singing source of pain or another.

Everything merged into an unseen rainbow of agony.

Then it was over. Clench rested both arms against the edge of his desk, breathing heavily. Howie leaned back against the side wall shaking his head with wonder, drops of sweat streaking from it as he did so. Ben squatted a few feet back from where Cuchillo lay, trying to steady his rasping breath.

As for the Apache, he didn't move.

It was for all the world as if he were dead.

And then it wasn't.

He pushed himself up from the floor and as he came up his right foot flashed out and caught the startled Ben under the jaw before he could as much as blink. As Ben's head jolted back and he lost balance, Cuchillo turned through a sweeping arc and his hands arrived at Clench. He got one powerful set of fingers tight round the lawman's neck and the other grasped his shirt front.

Clench was lifted bodily off his feet and swung round, lifted higher still and then sent slamming back against the wall.

Cuchillo turned again and saw Howie aiming his pistol. He threw himself across the desk in a rolling motion, sweeping everything off the surface and landing on his toes on the far side like a giant cat.

Howie fired and missed, fired and missed.

He cried out with anger and frustration, not knowing for certain where the Apache was.

Cuchillo lifted the desk on to his shoulders and charged towards the deputy with it held aloft before him.

Howie squeezed off one more shot, the wood splintering harmlessly away towards the ceiling. The desk top smashed into him, taking his face and chest and pulping them against the wall.

Cuchillo drew the heavy desk back and thrust it forwards once more. The bone at the center of the deputy's nose broke twice and noisily. Cartilage twisted and blood vessels ruptured. Cuchillo dropped the desk in time to catch Ben's arm as he came diving in. He pivotted on his heels and used the man's own momentum to send him crashing into the door. The woodwork shuddered and Ben shook all down his frame before falling unconscious to the floor.

That left Cuchillo and Sheriff Clench and the shotgun.

The sheriff was pushing himself groggily away from the wall and doing his best to focus on where exactly the Apache was. There was a lump at the back of his head the size of a goose's egg and he knew that it was steadily oozing blood.

He also knew that the gun was in the corner of the room, where it had been hurled when the desk was overturned.

Without the gun he didn't stand a chance.

He shook his head but it was still groggy. He didn't stand much of a chance anyway.

Another pace forward and he said, "Hey, now! Let's work something out here."

For a second it appeared that Cuchillo was considering it.

Clench dived for the shotgun.

Cuchillo let him make it. He let the sheriff's nervous, anxious fingers grasp the weapon at the second attempt and he let him make the turn. Then he let him have a straight-armed jab to the throat which closed off his throat and left him gasping for breath, eyes watering. He let him have a foot firmly between his legs and then a knee which crashed up to meet Clench's head as it jerked forward and down.

Clench screamed and thudded back against the wall. Blood and saliva sprayed from his mouth, heavily mixed with mucus and fragments of shattered tooth. His upper lip was cut where he'd bitten through it and blood was streaming from his already swollen nostrils. One eye looked at Cuchillo and the other was shut tight but neither was seeing a damned thing.

Back of him, Howie rolled over and the movement pushed the desk away from the wall. Cuchillo spun round but the deputy was no source of danger. He moved quickly towards him and drew the gold knife from his belt, sliding it down into his sheath.

Then he picked up the shotgun and held it above his head, bringing it down again and again against the edge of the desk until the stock had snapped clear and the barrels were mangled and bent.

He unlocked the door to the cells, using the sheriff's bunch of keys, and dragged the three men through from sight and locked them in one of the cells. He lifted up the table and set it to rights as well as he could. The mess of papers and such he kicked underneath. The longer he could keep the good citizens of Amigo from finding out what had happened to their law enforcement body the better chance he had of getting clear.

And getting clear meant getting to find Big Mitch Gresley.

Cuchillo opened the door and looked quickly both ways along the street. The gelding wasn't outside and it wasn't down by the store, so he guessed someone had been told to take it along to the livery barn. Anyway, that was where the Apache went to look and that was where he found it, blanket and sacks still in place, bridle still over the bay's head.

Cuchillo hushed the animal with a firm hand over his nose and pulled the .45 clear from the blanket and saw to loading five shells into the chamber. He pushed the pistol down into the front of his belt so that the butt was close to his left hand. He led the gelding to the barn door before slipping on to its back and setting off towards the edge of town the way he'd come in.

Someone over against the boardwalk shifted his head and raised a hand in a lazy gesture of greeting, called hello.

Cuchillo nodded, grunted, kept on going—just another friendly Amigo citizen anxious to pass the time of day.

As soon as he reached the board that marked the town boundary he flicked out with the rope that came from the gelding's bridle, kicked with his feet, and got away at a good gallop. It wasn't the kind of place that made a man want to linger.

Chapter Three

The ridge road looked down over the interlocking segments of the valley—a succession of hills which folded one into the other almost to the horizon. Here and there a clutter of pines or the occasional oak stood out hard and clear. Some fifty yards east from where Cuchillo was astride his horse, a batch of cottonwoods bent their heads in the direction of the ocean, miles behind. The purple heads of a hundred white thistles stared up from the ground, contrasting their color with the shades of tall, green grass. One of the nearest hills seemed to have been colonized by bright yellow mule ear, shifting lightly and as a mass with the wind.

The trading post was sheltered from both wind and sight, no more than three quarters of a mile away. Cuchillo had no way of knowing for certain that the man who had cheated him would be there, but it was the only place he had to start.

If anything worried him, it was going up against Mitch Gresley in front of maybe forty other white-eyes. They weren't the kind of odds that even a brave man went up against if he could avoid it. Cuchillo knew that he would have to weigh his anger against his common sense.

A bird moved into sudden flight from the nearest of the cottonwoods and he turned his head to watch it soar, silver-tipped wings catching the sun. When the bird had disappeared from sight, the Apache touched his feet to the bay's sides and moved slowly down into the valley.

Big Mitch Gresley was at the trading post, sure enough. He still had arrangements to make disposing of the load that Cuchillo had rescued from the desert. And there were other deals he was working on: a couple of dozen barrel loads of wine from Salinas Valley was being shipped down to San Francisco and some of it was bound from there to Portland; a consignment of Winchester .44-40s was on its way down from Sacramento to the Mexican border; a wagonload of whiskey from Kentucky was expected over the Sierras any day and there were arrangements to be made to have that watered down and bottled and sold.

Gresley had his fat, sticky fingers in a lot of sticky, fat pies.

Right now they were wrapped around a rack of lamb that he was holding in front of his face, gnawing the meat from the small, juicy bones. Grease was smeared all over his mouth, up into his thick mustache and down into the wiry hair of his beard. It ran down his fingers and into the palms of his hand, dripped on to the cuffs of his shirt and his pants and the table.

He chewed with his mouth partly open, as if he needed to breathe through his lips at the same time.

Life was pretty damned good! He'd got that consignment in from the desert without losing a thing and he hadn't even had to pay the fool Indian a cent for it—packing him off with that counterfeit money like he was paying him in cheap colored beads. Hell! Maybe next time that's what he'd do—go back to paying the fools in beads!

"Hey, Curly!" Gresley waved his arm at a bald-headed man sitting further along the trestle table. "I tell you 'bout the way I stung that fool injun with . . .?"

"Yeah, Mitch. You told me must be thirty-forty times already. Anyone'd think it was

some big deal the way you keep shootin'
your mouth off about it. All you did was
cheat him the way you cheat everybody else."

Curly laughed and four or five others joined
in. Mitch Gresley looked around and didn't
seem any too pleased to be made the butt of
someone else's humor.

He dropped what was left of his lamb chops
down onto the thick china plate and pointed
a thick finger at Curly. "You wanna watch
the way you let that tongue of yours run
around in your stupid mouth!"

Curly scraped back the stool he was sitting
on and angled himself round. He wasn't as
heavy as Mitch, but he was maybe five or so
years younger and he wasn't slow. He'd seen
Mitch in a bar room brawl down in San
Diego a year back. Mitch had nearly crushed
a man to death in a bear hug and the only
reason it hadn't happened was that four fellers dragged him away. Thing was, if the man
he'd got between his arms hadn't been more
or less a cripple, he wouldn't ever have got
hold of him in the first place. Put Mitch in a
straight race with most one-legged men he
could think of and Curly'd give odds on the
feller who was hopping.

Which meant he was about as scared of
Big Mitch as he was of a week-old rattler.

"You hear what I said about that mouth of

yours?" yelled Gresley, his anger even greater because of Curly's lack of response.

Curly scratched the top of his head and smiled: "Go fuck yourself!"

Mitch's mouth hung open and stayed that way long enough to have caught a couple of passing flies. Then he hammered one massive fist down on to the table and shook it off one set of trestles. A couple of plates slid to the straw-strewn floor and shattered across. A couple of men hollered annoyance and jumped to their feet. Down at the far end of the long room, Millie Caulson stopped measuring pinto beans into two pound sacks and slipped out to warn her husband, who was in the corral. If there was a danger of the place getting busted up, they wanted to be back there protecting whatever they could.

Mitch Gresley was squaring up to Curly like he'd take him apart with his bare hands, only Curly didn't seem bothered enough even to get up from his stool.

He just sat there, one leg crossed over the other, grinning up at Mitch and chewing at a piece of gristle that had got itself trapped between the few teeth he had left. He'd trapped up in the foothills of the Sierras for nigh-on ten years and he'd seen bears bigger than Mitch that hadn't made him shift ground when he was squatting down in the bushes relieving himself. He sure wasn't about to let Mitch worry him away from the best meal he'd had in a five-week.

"Get on your feet, Curly!"

Curly succeeded in freeing the piece of gristle and spat it down at Mitch's boots. It landed on the instep and stuck there. Mitch stared at it; stared at Curly's insolent face. There was a lot of laughter and all of it was directed at Big Mitch.

Big Mitch didn't like it.

He charged at Curly and his arms reached forward to grab him and squeeze the life plumb out of him.

For a couple of seconds it looked as if he was going to succeed and then it didn't. All he caught between his arms was air as Curly sprang sideways out of his way. The stool rapped painfully against Mitch's shins and he stumbled ten yards before pitching down onto his face.

When he rolled over his front was covered in straw and spit and bits of uneatable food that had been thrown down and left by the half dozen mongrel dogs that the Caulson's kept on the place.

Old Man Caulson was back at the store counter resting his Remington sawn-off underneath a piece of old sacking, finger resting anxious against the twin triggers.

"You're dead, you miserable bastard!" shouted Mitch from the floor. "You're dead!"

"If I'm the one who's dead," said Curly with a laugh, "how come you're the one who's lyin' down?"

Men hollered and banged the table and stomped their feet.

Curly spread his legs and held his balance and waited for the charge he knew must come.

Mitch was up off the floor like a wounded buffalo.

Curly again waited until the last moment and sidestepped, only this time he didn't get it exactly right. Mitch's left shoulder drove into his back and sent him sprawling into the table, taking it right off the trestles and flat onto the floor. Curly skidded with it some dozen feet, taking a couple of onlookers with him.

More plates and knives bounced noisily around and in the midst of all that clamor, Mitch roared like a wild animal on the rampage.

Curly pushed himself on to his hands and knees, winded. He was half way into a turn when Mitch's knee caught him on the upper arm and numbed it to the bone.

Curly fell back and kicked out with his foot. The toe got Mitch full in the stomach and it was as if nothing had happened. He simply kept on coming. Mitch cannoned into Curly and drove him down against the table, lifting him up by his neck and butting him full in the face with his head.

Curly's head swum in a sea of colored, shifting lights and he knew without feeling it with his hand that his nose was broken. Blood splattered all down the front of his buckskin shirt. He put out a hand to ward off Mitch's advance and Mitch bit through three fingers right to the bone.

Curly screamed and then he was tight in Mitch's arms and his breath was being squeezed out of him.

He struggled and kicked and tried his best to extricate himself but he knew that he was getting weaker and he didn't have long. He snorted into Mitch's face and covered the fat-clogged beard with mucus and blood but that didn't stop the shine of triumph in Mitch's small, dark eyes.

Curly slid backwards and managed to bring one thigh up hard enough between the big man's legs to make him wince; he did it a second time and Mitch's balance was gone. They hit the floor with an almighty crash and rolled over and over until they came to a halt against the wall. Mitch still had his arms wrapped around Curly and all that Curly had been able to achieve was to free one arm.

"You're dead!" gasped Mitch, muscles straining for the final effort that would rupture Curly's blood vessels, burst his lungs, crack more of the already broken ribs.

"You're dead!"

Curly gasped and clawed with his fingers and scooped a fork from where it had fallen. He wriggled and turned and as he was moaning for air he managed to bring the fork over the top of the big man's arm.

Mitch held his breath and tightened his finger grip at Curly's back just as the three prongs of the fork, still greasy with meat, jabbed into the corner of his eye.

The effect was instantaneous.

Big Mitch screamed and let go of his hold. He swung his head away and the fork gouged three lines down through his cheek. He roared and the fork drove into his ear and ripped through an inch of gristle and loose flesh.

Curly jumped sideways, landing a heel in Mitch's belly on the way.

He hurled the fork aside and ran hard as he could for the opposite wall, close by the main door. It wasn't the door he was heading for. There were pegs fastened in the wood to either side and from one of these hung Curly's hide coat. Underneath the coat, dangling from its strap, was his Sharps rifle.

He fumbled the coat free, caught hold of the rifle and turned.

Big Mitch was lumbering towards him, like a wounded bear.

Curly knew there wasn't a shell in the chamber but he hoped Mitch didn't. "Hold it!" he called, aiming the rifle at Mitch's middle. "Come another yard and I'll blow a hole right through you."

Mitch didn't know the rifle was unloaded; he might have suspected it but he wasn't about to take that risk. He'd seen what a Sharps could do to a deer, even a bear; he could guess what it would do to a man from that close range and he knew Curly wasn't about to miss.

Old Man Caulson shrugged the sawn-off out from under the piece of sacking and came out from back of the counter. "Let's have an end to it," he said, gesturing with the gun first to one man and then the other. "No point in either one of you endin' up dead."

Curly was still fightin to regain some rhythm in his breathing. He figured he'd have to get his ribs taped good and that the next three months in the saddle were going to hurt like hell. But the sight of blood streaming from several places on Mitch's face gave

him a powerful satisfaction and he reckoned
Caulson was right. Whatever had been the
start of the fight, it weren't worth dyin' for.

"How 'bout it, Mitch?"

"How 'bout what?" Mitch growled.

"Shakin' hands, I guess."

Gresley shook his head instead and spat.

"Shake on it," said Old Man Caulson and
he levelled the shotgun at Mitch's side.

The combination of shotgun and Sharps
changed Mitch Gresley's mind. He shrugged
forward and held out a paw of a hand, looking anywhere but into Curly's face.

Curly managed a smile and he lowered the
rifle and gripped the hand.

"C'mon over," said Caulson, "whiskey on
the house."

He poured two stiff shots of liquor and
gave the glasses to the two men, ordering
them to drink up and forget their differences.

"Sure," said Curly and lifted his glass towards Mitch in a toast before sinking its contents in one.

Mitch half-heartedly repeated the gesture,
drank the whiskey in a couple of swallows
and lumbered away to get his face washed
up.

"You watch your back from now on,"
warned Caulson as soon as Gresley was out

of earshot. "Mitch ain't the kind of feller to forget a grudge."

"Don't you worry none," grinned Curly, "he ain't goin' to get that close to me again ever."

Curly was wrong. Eight months later, stepping out back of the cantina in Los Padres and opening his pants front with numb fingers to take a piss, he would hear another sound intrude upon the warm hiss that was melting the snow before him.

Curly would shake himself quickly dry and begin to turn in time to catch the jagged end of a broken bottle at full thrust in the face. He would barely recognize Mitch Gresley through the welter of bright blood, barely see the wide hunting knife that drove up through his thick hide coat and penetrated his chest, seeking a route between his ribs and finding it at the third attempt.

Curly's last choked spumes of blood would glisten like sudden comets in the moonlight before staining the snow a dull, dying red.

Right now he didn't know that.

Right now he laughed and clapped Old Man Caulson on the shoulder and called for another shot.

Right now Cuchillo was riding slow and easy towards the trading post from the northeast.

He could see there were still some dozen and a half mounts in the corral out back, another four tied up to one of the long stretches of hitching rail at the front. He thought he recognized the black mare that Big Mitch Gresley rode but he wasn't sure.

At the edge of the corral he dismounted and turned the reins about the corner post a few times. The .45 was sticking up from his belt and he knew it was loaded. The triangular blade was in its sheath at his back. The front door to the post was fifteen yards away, the back door closer.

He headed for the back.

He was stepping like a ghost towards the door when it swung open and he was face to face with Old Man Caulson.

Caulson's mouth fell open, the sack of potatoes shifted on his shoulder. He didn't recognize Cuchillo as the Indian who'd done business with Gresley—just knew him as an Indian.

"What the hell you sneakin' round here fer?"

"Not sneaking. Coming into post."

"Yeah?" sneered Caulson. "Then you use the front door like everyone else. Sneakin' round here to steal like all your kind!"

Caulson saw the pistol and Cuchillo's belt and started to feel less than comfortable. He shot a quick glance over his shoulder and considered yelling.

He was too slow, too old, too late.

Cuchillo's pistol was reversed in his left hand and the butt came crashing down against the side of his head, smashing into the bone immediately in front of his left ear.

Old Man Caulson sighed and slumped against the wall by the door, Cuchillo catching him and laying him down close by the fallen sack of potatoes.

The Apache slipped inside the rear door and took his bearings. He was standing in a store room, sacks of onions and potatoes and flour, crates and barrels stacked one upon the other. Through the open door he could see the long iron range of the kitchen, Caulson's wife kneading dough. Beyond that was the main room of the post. Voices filtered through, words blurred and joined together.

Cuchillo got to within five feet of Millie before instinct rather than sound made her turn her head. She was midway into her scream when the Apache's mutilated hand clapped fast over her mouth. Her eyes, terrified, stared at him from above the hand as her slender, aging body kicked and struggled.

Cuchillo wanted to warn her to keep silent, tell her that he meant her no harm. He knew it was a waste of time. He grunted and laid the long barrel of the .45 alongside her temple and felt her slump unconscious against him.

He let her slide through his arms and curl on to the kitchen floor. There was no sign of anyone inside the post having heard the beginnings of her scream.

Cuchillo moved stealthily to the inner door.

Five men were playing cards round a circular table close by the counter. Another two were playing dominoes near the window towards the front door. Three others were spread along the trestle table, eating. The straw across the floor had been pushed into untidy heaps and there were other signs of upheaval, as if maybe there recently been some kind of fight.

Cuchillo peered around the interior, unable to figure out if Big Mitch Gresley was one of the men. He was just deciding that he wasn't when the front door opened and the big man came through. Immediately, Cuchillo saw that if there had been a fight, then Gresley had been at the heart of it. One side of his face was badly scratched and scarred, the lobe of his ear seemed to be hanging on by no more than a sliver of skin.

The Apache grinned, giving his thanks to whoever had softened Gresley up for him. He watched as the man who had cheated him turned and walked over to the group of poker players, watched for a few moments, and then went slowly to the counter, leaning one arm down on it and calling for a drink.

Cuchillo's smile grew—neither of the Caulsons was about to come out and serve him. He wondered how patient Gresley would be. A couple of shouts and a bang on the table more or less answered the question for him. After that he was lurching towards the kitchen to find out why the hell he wasn't getting any service.

Cuchillo stepped back behind the door and let the angry man come through.

"Shut the door!" Cuchillo hissed.

Mitch Gresley spun pretty fast for a big man who'd been in one hell of a fight not more than half an hour before. He saw Cuchillo and saw the gun in his hand and the air seemed to go out of him like a deflated balloon.

"Shut it!"

Gresley stretched out his hand and pushed it closed.

"What the fuck d'you reckon you're doin' here, you bastard?"

The grin on Cuchillo's face was broad. "And you say Cuchillo Oro like a white man."

"Like fuck!"

Cuchillo was still grinning as he pistol-whipped the white man across the side of his face—the side that Curly had left untouched.

Gresley went staggering back into a table and Cuchillo followed up with a second slashing blow which ripped a couple of inches of flesh loose from the corner of Gresley's mouth.

When he cursed Cuchillo blood bubbled from between his lips.

"You cheat me!" Cuchillo said, moving in close.

"I paid you every damn cent. . . ."

"You pay with bad money. I want good money. Now."

"I don't have no more money."

"You lie!"

"No! I don't have. . . ."

The end of the .45 was tight against Gresley's forehead and it wasn't wavering as much as an inch.

"Get! Get money!"

"I told you, you mad bastard, I don't have no money."

Cuchillo stepped back and the grin slid back on to his face. He looked at the big hands Gresley was gesturing with, saw the gold ring shining on the middle finger of the right hand.

"Give me ring!"

Gresley shook his head, slapped the hand down on the edge of the table and gripped it tight. "That ring's worth more'n you alive or dead."

Cuchillo moved more swiftly than Gresley could follow. He struck him full in the face with the underside of the pistol barrel and then the .45 was back in his belt and the glimmering knife was high in his hand.

Mitch Gresley was slumped back against the table, struggling not to lose consciousness. His hand still gripped the table.

Cuchillo drove the point of the knife through the middle of Big Mitch Gresley's hand.

Gresley screamed.

Cuchillo punched him low in the belly and slapped the back of his hand across his pained face.

The knife was still pinning his hand to the table, blood beginning to well up around it and run down between the trapped fingers.

"Money!" yelled Cuchillo.

Gresley shook his head.

Cuchillo used his right side to slam Gresley back against the table and hold him there. He drew the knife up from the trapped hand with a quick sucking sound and sent it plunging back down, its target changed.

The thick blade pressed against the bone of Gresley's middle finger and as the big man shrieked out in agony, Cuchillo leaned all of his weight down onto the blade.

The bone splintered across and the finger flew across the kitchen, bouncing against the far wall and dropping down close by the curled, unconscious body of Millie Caulson.

Cuchillo swooped down and picked it up, holding it before Gresley's scarred, scared face.

"You got no money, I take ring."

The Apache pulled the gold ring off the finger end and dropped it into his pants pocket. Men were hammering on the kitchen door, shouting. Cuchillo came close to Gresley and rammed his knee between his legs; as the big man bent forward, vomiting, Cuchillo neatly slipped the finger into the center of his mouth.

"Bite on that!"

Shoulders charged against the door. Millie Caulson stirred. Cuchillo ran for the back door. He came face to face with Old Man Caulson, groggily getting to his feet. Cuchillo elbowed him aside and back to the ground. He sprinted towards the corner of the corral and he was half way there when he realized that the gelding was gone.

Cuchillo pulled up short, shot a glance over his shoulder.

Pursuit was at hand.

He vaulted over the corral fence and leapt on to the back of a gray mare with white fetlocks and a high, arching tail. He caught tight hold of the mare's mane and rode her between the other horses, picking up speed. With stray bullets trying to seek him out, he galloped the gray at the corral fence and jumped her clear with ease, flattening himself on her back and leaving the trading post swiftly in his wake.

Chapter Four

The trail had been easy to follow. First off,
Cuchillo had taken care to lose the half-
hearted pursuit that had galloped after him
from the trading post. Then he had back-
tracked and picked up the trail of the gelding. Whoever was riding it was light, light
enough to be a woman, either that or a youth.
He drove the horse hard at first, covering the
mile or so up from the valley at careless
speed. Once on the rim, he—or she—had
clearly felt safer and had allowed the bay to
choose its own pace.

So Cuchillo followed the hoofprints for a
couple of hours, not bothering to drive the
mare harder and catch the thief before time
naturally brought them together. He was in
no great hurry and, besides, he was curious
as to the thief's reasons for taking the gelding

as opposed to any other; he wanted to know
the why and the where of it.

The where seemed to be a one-eyed place
named Jackson Crossing.

Maybe twenty or more years back the creek
had been wider and faster flowing. Right now
there was little more than a trickle and the
old flat-bed ferry was stranded on a slope of
sand like a boat that had been beached and
forgotten by the tide. There were half a dozen
buildings in no real formation around the
crossing—a couple of adobes and the rest ram-
shackle places nailed together from whatever
bits and ends of material had come to hand.
It wasn't a ghost town though—a few horses
stood disconsolately in a corral at the far
side of the creek, pigs and chickens were
penned up against one of the adobes. Smoke
drifted lazily from the tin chimney of one of
the shacks and posed against the flat blue
wash of the sky.

Cuchillo saw the gelding right off. It was
tethered to a post outside the adobe with the
pigs and chickens. There was no sign of whoever had taken it.

Cuchillo waited high on the creek bed for
a while but no one appeared and he decided
there wasn't anything to lose by riding down
to the settlement. It didn't look as if it held

any special danger, but then he knew better than trust appearances.

He was fifty yards from the central adobe when a Winchester poked through a crack in the side wall of one of the shacks and a voice hollered for him to rein in and stay where he was.

Cuchillo saw the swift glint of the rifle barrel in the sunlight and did as he was told.

A full minute later, the Winchester still covering him, a woman with gray hair and wearing a flowered apron over a blue and green print dress came out of the front of the shack. She had a Colt Frontier held in both hands and the butt was hauled back against her stomach. If she pulled against the trigger it would likely kick her in the guts like an angry mule.

Cuchillo hoped she wasn't about to pull the trigger.

"What's your business here?" said the woman, squinting against the light.

Cuchillo shook his head. "Passing through."

"Through to where?"

"West."

The woman paused, glanced towards the shack. The rifle was steady against the planking. Further back into the settlement there were folk stirring—a couple of men appeared at the back of the second adobe—the one

with the stock—and shuffled their way ca-
gily up the slope towards Cuchillo and the
woman. At the front of another shack, an
old-timer brandishing a broom handle did
his best to look threatening.

Cuchillo wondered what had happened to
give the citizens of Jackson's Crossing such a
wary opinion of strangers. They were about
as friendly and welcoming as the good folk
of Amigo.

"West's a big place," commented the woman.

Cuchillo shrugged. "Only riding through.
Don't want trouble. Nothing."

The woman swung her head as the two
men came close behind her. One of them
had a pistol tucked down into his belt, the
butt towards his hand; the other didn't seem
to be armed, but, again, that didn't necessar-
ily mean a whole lot.

The gelding was still by the hitching post
and no one had made a move towards it.
Cuchillo didn't figure that any of those
around him was the one who'd stolen his
horse.

The Winchester drew in from the wall and
a few moments later it appeared again held
in the gnarled hands of a stoop-backed man
with a shock of white hair. He wasn't all that
old—more like something had aged him be-

fore his time and left him stooped and white, like a tree struck by a bolt of lightning.

"We had us a bunch of fellers a time back," the stoop-backed man said in a slow drawl "coupla Indians among 'em. They was just passin' through. Afore they left they raped. . . ."

"Henry!" the woman with gray hair protested, but he waved her aside impatiently.

"They raped young Arlene from the Foster place and she was a couple of months short of her fifteenth birthday. Stole every cent any of us had and took the best part of our supplies for the comin' winter." He eased a mouthful of phlegm out on to the end of his tongue and spat it lazily down at the ground. "So now whenever anyone rides through, specially when he sits up the creek for a time before makin' up his mind, we act a mite more careful than we did before."

Cuchillo nodded his head. "I understand. I am no thief. I. . . ."

"I know, you're ridin' through," said the man.

"Headin' west," said the woman.

The pistol at the third man's belt was resting against his hand now.

Cuchillo had his own .45 pushed down into the middle of his pants belt and the knife was in its usual place at his back. He didn't want to risk a fight with these people if it could be avoided.

But then he did want his horse back.

"How come you was sittin' up there spyin' out the place so long?" asked the stooped man from back of his Winchester. "Seems strange for a man who ain't figurin' on gettin down off his horse to do."

Cuchillo pointed beyond them to where the gelding was standing, one of the chickens pecking the dirt close to his feet. "That horse," he said.

"How 'bout it?" asked the man with the pistol a little too quickly.

Cuchillo stared at him long enough to get the hand moved away from the butt of the gun. "It's mine."

The stooped man spat and nodded towards the animal Cuchillo was astride. "How 'bout that?"

"A man can own two horses."

"Maybe."

"The bay, it is mine."

The man stood forward from the back, fidgeting with his belt. "You seem awful sure of that. You don't reckon as how you could be mistaken now, do you?"

"No mistake."

"You sure you. . . ."

"No mistake!"

Everyone was getting a real nervous look in their eyes and there was a lot of shifting of hands over weapons and a lot of glances passed back and forth.

"Who rode horse here?" Cuchillo asked.

The men looked at one another, but no one spoke.

"Who rode horse here is thief," said Cuchillo. His voice was firm and strong and against its sureness the men faltered. The woman kept the pistol pressed against her body but it was easy to tell from the expression on her face that she was no longer certain as to the rightness of what they were doing.

Cuchillo pointed at them, one after the other with a sweep of his hand. "You stole horse?"

The man with the white hair and the bent back got riled about being called a horse thief by an Indian and went off at the mouth some, but no one else said a thing. Cuchillo guessed they knew what he was saying to be true and that they were protecting someone.

And then he saw who.

The boy came out of the same building the two men had come from, kicking out at one of the hens when it got too near to his boot. He set himself close to the gelding and wiped his arm across his forehead, shifting a falling lock of fair hair away from his eyes. He was fifteen, maybe sixteen, slender and with a strength that had yet to thicken out and take on substance. His face was oval and handsome, his eyes a bright blue that seemed to reflect the sky. His mouth was full and red and his fair hair was worn long enough to rest against his shoulders.

He was wearing a pale blue shirt and patched denim pants and his boots were worn and scuffed.

The pistol in his right hand was a short-barrelled Colt and the hammer was back against his slender thumb.

It was aiming up the slope towards where Cuchillo sat astride the gray.

His voice was clear and light. "I took your horse."

"Why?"

"I needed it."

"Why my horse?"

"Only one weren't in the corral or tied up out front. I needed it in a hurry."

"You always steal what you want?"

The boy's upper lip curled into a sneer. "You sure talk a lot for an Indian."

"White man teach me his tongue."

The man with the pistol at his belt had turned back towards the youth. "You never said you stole the mount, Marty."

The sneer became a scowl. "I never figured it to matter."

The man glanced round at Cuchillo, then at the boy. "Now you can see how it does."

The youngster raised his gun arm meaningfully. "It don't have to."

"You take care, Marty!" called the woman. "Marty, don't be a fool!"

Cuchillo slid his fingers around the butt of his pistol and waited to see what the boy would do. At that range it would be a lucky shot that would drop the Apache from the gray's back, but he'd rather it was no shot at all.

"He ain't nothin' but an' injun an' a horse thief!"

"You the thief!" retorted Cuchillo.

Marty laughed, but there was no humor in the sound. "I'm the thief, how come you're sittin' on another man's horse? I saw you come sneakin' up to that tradin' post just like you did here. You never had no two mounts then, an' that's a fact. You stole that gray an' you can't deny it."

"I steal horse," said Cuchillo, angry, "because you steal mine first."

"Two wrongs don't make a right," said the woman, but no one paid her any heed.

"I come after you, get my horse back," snarled Cuchillo, ignoring the rest of them.

Marty held his pistol steady. "You want the horse, injun, you just better come get it."

Cuchillo did just that and the speed with which he moved startled the youngster into wasting a couple of shots high over the Apache's head. Cuchillo had kicked suddenly into the gray's sides and sent it plunging down the slope towards the youth, leaning low over the animal's neck and presenting as small a target as possible.

The rest jumped back out of the way, the sudden surge forward catching them by surprise, the mare catching one of the men a glancing blow and setting him down on his back with a thump and a holler.

Cuchillo was upon the youngster before he could squeeze off a third shot. He dived from the speeding animal's back and brought the kid to the ground with a crash. Chickens flew squawking into the air and came down in a flurry of indignation and feathers.

A fist punched against the side of the Apache's head but he shrugged it away and threw the kid over on to his back, twisting the gun arm high between his shoulder blades.

Marty yelled out and his fingers opened, the Colt spilling out.

Cuchillo snatched it from the ground and hurled it down towards the creek. He snaked his arm tight about the kid's neck and pulled him on to his knees. In a flash the knife was out of his sheath and tight in his other hand, the triangular blade glinting against the smooth skin of Marty's youthful throat.

"Stay!" Cuchillo shouted to the men advancing down the slope towards them. "Stay or. . . ."

But there was no need for him to fill in the details of his threat. It was plain enough for them all to see—plain in the fear that rose in the youngster's blue eyes and in the way his skin was taut against the gold of the Apache's blade.

"Stay!" Cuchillo repeated.

But they had already stayed.

"Throw down weapons!"

Grudgingly they did as they were told.

Sweat trickled down from Marty's face on to his neck and on to Cuchillo's arm, ran from there on to the blade of the knife beneath.

"In this country," said Cuchillo slowly, "man who steals horse of another deserve to die."

The boy imagined the knife slashing his neck open like a wolf's hungry fangs.

"Let him tell you!" called the woman. "Let him tell you why he done it. Then you'll see. Then you'll understand."

Cuchillo looked at her angrily. Why should

he listen to excuses? A stolen horse was a stolen horse. If he had not been quick-witted enough, quick and agile enough of limb, then the boy's theft of the gelding could have caused Cuchillo's death.

He felt the youth shake against him, the mighty knife still tight against his bared throat.

"Let him go," urged the man with the Winchester. "She's right. Let him tell his tale. Then if you still feel the same. . . ."

Cuchillo looked at him expectantly.

"Well, if you still feel the same, do what you gotta do. We ain't goin' to stop you."

Cuchillo hesitated. He could almost feel life surging back into the boy's veins. He nodded towards the man who had spoken last. "Take all weapons. Leave them aside. Then I release the boy. Then he will talk. After that, I will decide."

When it was done, Cuchillo pulled the knife clear off the youth's throat and held it in front of him while he released his arm from beneath his chin. Marty rubbed at his throat, wincing and trying hard not to show his fear. The woman asked permission to fetch him water, went into the nearest place and returned with a cup.

The stoop-backed man moved to help the boy to his feet but he shook him off and got awkwardly to his feet himself, still gingerly feeling the marks on his neck where the Apache had gripped him tight. He stood out of the sun, taking the shade of the adobe, his voice less than certain at the beginning, growing in strength and anger as his story neared its end.

"I was travelling west, out through California towards the ocean. Me and Natalie. Her folks had been killed in a flash flood and she didn't have no other kin. She weren't but fourteen." He said it as though he was a lot more than sixteen himself. "I figured if we went west as far as we could go we could make a new start. There's all kinds of good land out there, rich. I ain't talkin' 'bout gold, but crops an' fruit and such. And besides," he smiled, "I always wanted to see the ocean. So did Natalie. She wanted to see it more than anything."

He paused and wiped his forehead, leaving a deep smear mark from his arm.

"We got as far as the edge of the desert and one of the horses we was ridin' bust a leg. There wasn't nothin' but to shoot him. Natalie, she cried a lot about that but she weren't no more'n a slip of a thing and we got along on one horse okay. Things we was taking was tied on a travois behind us. . . ." He glanced at Cuchillo. ". . . like we was Indians."

He stopped again, looking apprehensively

around—this was the part of the tale he didn't want to retell.

"We come upon this waterin' hole and Natalie she wanted to take a bath. Jumped in the water like she was still a little kid. Splashin' and shriekin' an' such." He kicked at the dust with his heel. "She was still in the water when they rode up. They come fast an' there weren't no time to pull her out or get her covered or nothin'."

Marty's blue eyes passed from one face to another, as if seeking their assurance that there was nothing else that he could have done.

"Go on with it, Marty," the gray-haired woman said softly.

Marty nodded towards the ground. "There was eight of 'em. Breeds an' a couple of Indians, some of 'em white as you or me." Again, he flicked a nervous glance towards Cuchillo, but the Apache's face remained impassive. "They fooled around at first, cheerin' her an' making jokes like it was all a piece of fun." He shook his head and there were tears at the back of his eyes. "It weren't no fun. They dragged her out and when I tried to stop them they smashed a rifle butt in my face and tied me up. I weren't conscious, not most of the time, but I could hear her screams

and their laughter and then Natalie screamin'
again."

Marty pushed himself away from the adobe
wall and walked a few paces along the side
of the building.

"Go on, Marty," said the woman, "tell the
rest."

He nodded, caught his breath, continued.
"When I come to she wasn't nowhere to be
seen. Nor was any of the gang. No horse. No
weapons. No food. I was left out there without a damned thing other than what I stood
up in an' Natalie had been taken. Taken and
the Lord knows what else. Anyway, I headed
out after 'em on foot. They hadn't bothered
none to hide their tracks. They knew that
even if I come after 'em there weren't any
way I was goin' to catch 'em up on foot."

He looked around defiant, almost proud.

"I did what I could. Stole food from one
place, a gun from another. First off I stole a
mule an' then a broken-down old mare and
she gave up and died under me, her damned
old heart just give out. I asked questions
wherever I got the chance. Seems the bunch
was led by a feller named Jake McCoy. Some
reckoned they still had a girl with 'em and
some didn't, but I kept right on after 'em
anyhow. I was gettin' pretty close one time
and then I lost 'em altogether. Out at that

tradin' post I heard they'd come this way a couple of weeks back."

The stoop-backed man interrupted: "They was here right enough and they had a slip of a girl with 'em. Hair black like a raven an' eyes big as I ever seen afore. They robbed and cussed and like I said before they raped Arlene Foster. Most the whole damned bunch of 'em." He cleared his throat down into the dirt. "Arlene an' this girl they had with 'em, they was close to the same age." He didn't look at Marty when he said that.

Marty knew only too well what he meant; he could remember the shrill tearing screams between the raucous laughter.

He went on: "That was when I stole your horse. I needed to get out here to Jackson's Crossing soon as I could. Course, all I found was they'd been here an' were long gone." He shrugged his shoulders, straightened his back and looked out at the rest, as if daring any of them to defy him. "Now I'm goin' on after 'em again. I'll catch them bastards up one day, if it takes me most of my life."

Cuchillo stared at him. He was brave but he was foolish. He remembered the young men of his tribe, thirsting to prove themselves. He said: "When you find them they will kill you."

"I got to find Natalie."

"She will be dead."

"No!"

He rushed at Cuchillo and the Apache stepped swiftly aside and tripped the youth, sending him sprawling.

"How long you think they carry her around? One month, two? When she is no longer amusement for them, they throw her aside like old meat chewed over too many times."

The gray-haired woman covered her face with her hands and turned aside.

"You catch them, they kill you sure. If girl not dead yet she will die then." Cuchillo shook his head. "Leave her. Leave them. Forget."

Marty pushed himself to his feet and squared up to the Apache. David to Goliath. "I ain't never goin' to forget. Not ever. Maybe you're the kind who can forget somethin' like this, but not me. Not me."

He turned away, tears of impotence and rage blurring his vision. Cuchillo looked at his back, smoldering under his words. Forget—the kind of man who would forget! How many nights did he fall asleep with his woman's name on his lips and wake with her arms around him, only to find with the first flush of light that she had slipped away from him again, back to the land where she walked and waited? How many times did he turn at his child's voice and realize too late that it was the cry of the wind in the pines?

Forget!

He strode through the watchers and stood alongside the youth. "You will take the gray mare. I will ride the gelding. We will ride together. And together we will find these men. Find the girl."

Marty stared at the Apache, unable to believe the words; not understanding the reasons behind them.

His mouth opened to ask the question, but Cuchillo stopped him with a quick gesture of the hand.

"If there are things to say, let them be said later. Now there is much riding to do, many miles to travel. And time is not our friend."

He set his hand for a moment on the boy's shoulder.

"Come!"

Marty hesitated no more than a moment, then followed.

Chapter Five

Jake McCoy and his bunch of desperadoes swathed a bloody trail across Southern California, leaving widows and bereft fathers in their wake. They rode up to the Delaney place late one night, the clouds full of rain and the stars little more than a glimmer tracing dreams across the sky. They asked if they could hole up in the grain barn, offered to pay a fee for lodging, Jake McCoy shook Delaney's hand and promised him they'd be clear by morning and he'd never know they'd been there. As lies went it was pretty strong.

Except the part about leaving by morning: that much was true.

For the rest, it was doubtful if anyone on the place would forget that they'd been granted a visitation—none of those, that is, who were left alive to remember anything.

It began when McCoy's right hand man, a slant-eyed gunhawk called Nevada, drained the last bottle of rotgut whiskey they had with them and hurled the bottle against the barn wall, smashing it to smithereens.

He had the kind of thirst that wasn't easily assuaged and that night more than most he was not to be denied. He called for Lopez and Juan to go with him and together they lurched over to the main building.

Mrs. Delaney had just finished washing up the supper things and her thirteen year old daughter was helping her to stack things away. Her son was in the living room playing checkers with his father. The two hands were already in the bunk house, one of them stitching the leather of his gunbelt and the other darning a pair of wool socks that smelt so strong he had to hold them well clear of his nose before he could handle them at all.

When the three men came blustering in demanding something to drink, Mrs. Delaney controlled her anger and fear and shushed the girl, pretending that she didn't notice the way Nevada looked at her growing breasts beneath her apron.

She offered them a bottle of wine and when one of the Mexicans snatched it and glowered at her with an expression which said, you don't reckon you're getting off that lightly?, she walked calm as she could from the kitchen to the living room.

"Ned, our guests here would like something to drink. I wonder if you could get some of that wine from the cupboard?"

Delaney read the meaning that showed in his wife's face if not her words. He could see the three men behind her, all of them looking as though they'd already drunk more than enough. He was only too aware of the dangers to his son and daughter, to say nothing of themselves.

"Sure, be glad to."

The shotgun was on the shelf inside the cupboard and he knew there was a charge of 0-0 shot ready in place. His breathing was rapid as he stepped towards the cupboard and his fingers were far from still. He walked slow as he could, not wanting to give the intruders any sign of trouble.

The key turned easy in the door and he stepped inside the tall cupboard. His hands were sweating on the grip of the gun, slippery on the stock and trigger. Sweat was running down his temples, thick at his groin and beneath his arms. He thought they must be able to smell the high stink of it.

Delaney turned fast as he could and came back into the room with the hammers cocked and the shotgun covering all three men.

Guessing what was to happen, his wife
had taken her time crossing the room to where
the boy was sitting and had put her hand
gently on his shoulder. As soon as her husband emerged she gripped him tight and kept
him still.

"I told you you could spend the night in
the barn out of the storm," Delaney said, his
voice barely controlled. "I should've known
better than to give way to trash. Now you
can get out of my house and off my property
and the first one as tries anything'll get a
bellyful of this."

Delaney pushed the shotgun a few inches
closer and all that Jake McCoy's men did
was laugh. Nevada poked his finger in the
farmer's direction and said: "You wanna be
careful with toys like that when you ain't
used to 'em. Might go off in your face."

"This goes off in anyone's face it'll be yours.
Now get off my property and tell the rest of
that rabble out there the first one as shows
his face again'll get it full of buckshot!"

Nevada grinned and shrugged. "C'mon,
boys."

He turned towards the door and the Mexicans followed suit. Delaney glanced quickly
at his wife and as he did so he realized that
his daughter was not there. She was still in
the kitchen.

Doubt flooded his face and it was smacked into certainty by the girl's scream.

Nevada thrust her through the living room door with a pistol to her head. The girl's face was pale, trembling; she seemed suddenly to have aged beyond even her mother's years. Perhaps it was a sense of her own mortality.

"Now you can throw down the gun," smiled Nevada crookedly.

Delaney hesitated uncertain. If he did as he was told, it would be the end for all of them—but if he tried to shoot his way out then his child would die at his own hands even if the gunman didn't put a bullet through her brain.

"Ned!"

His wife's voice made up his mind for him—that and the haunted look in the girl's terror-stricken eyes.

He released the triggers and held the shotgun out to one side. One of the Mexicans came forward and took it from him with a grin. He broke the gun and checked that it was loaded; still grinning, he snapped it back again and swung it round till the barrel-ends were hard against the farmer's ribs.

"Get on your knees!"

The second Mexican forced the woman into the same position. When the boy tried to struggle with him, he was booted in the chest and punched in the head for his pains. He lay in the corner, wimpering.

Nevada released the hammer on his Colt and slipped it back down into his holster.

The girl was shaking so much she could scarcely comply with the simplest of his requests.

The Mexican used the shotgun to compel both parents to watch.

When it was over the first time, Nevada ordered her out to the barn to where Jake and the rest of the gang were waiting. This time they took the mother too. Delaney was knocked unconscious with the shotgun stock and only the smell of smoke and the crackle of flames brought him round.

The main building was on fire. He managed to drag himself and the boy to safety, shouting all the time for his wife and daughter. They were out back of the grain barn, torn and bleeding, too ashamed to look one another in the face. Shamed by the guilt of others and not themselves.

The flames grew and licked around the outbuildings. They flickered high into the night and only the advent of the promised storm left anything of the Delaney place from becoming ashes and cinder.

By that time Jake McCoy and his gang were long gone.

* * *

They surfaced next in a middling town called San Pietro. Originally it had been a Spanish mission and the old mission building still stood at the edge of the town, gnarled pepper trees either side of the adobe arched gateway. The bell tower had begun to crumble away and no bell had hung there for sixty or more years. Sheep wandered in and out of the courtyard and sheltered against the excessive sun or the sudden rains.

San Pietro had a new church and a windmill, farms and prosperity. It had a branch of the Southern California Assay and Banking Company situated right across the broad dusty street from the Silver Dollar saloon.

McCoy and the bulk of his men spent a couple of hours sprawled at the tables in the saloon, getting steadily drunker and drunker. A few of them played a little poker and Nevada tried to rouse the town whore into some action, but generally it was a lazy afternoon.

Only when a short Apache with thick greasy hair and a foul temper got into an argument with the barkeep did things liven up any. Bitter Moon drew a double-edged knife from his belt and warned the man that if he didn't serve up some decent whiskey instead of goat-piss, he'd cut off his right ear.

The Apache was so drunk by that time, he

could have had any damned liquor at all and
not known what the hell he was drinking.
The barkeep was on to a loser all the way.
Bitter Moon smashed the glass by hurling it
against a row of bottles back of the counter.
Then he jumped up onto the bar, making it
at the second attempt, wrested the man's pistol away from him and slashed down with
his knife. He took off the ear neater than he
should have been able and the fact that it
was the left and not the right was solely due
to the Apache never having learned the
difference.

One of the townsfolk thought to interfere
and Nevada laughed and put a bullet through
his leg, just above the kneecap.

After that there didn't seem to be anything
else to do but take the bank.

There were only five people inside at the
time: the manager and two of his staff, a
short-sighted woman whose spectacles dangled from thin black ribbon round her neck
and a pimply youth who was learning how
to cast columns of figures and hoping to make
a name for himself in the banking business—
one customer and a drunk looking for a
sheltered place to sleep.

When McCoy's bunch burst in the manager made a dash for his office desk, wanting

to get his hand on the shiny new Colt .45 he'd bought for just such an emergency.

Nevada let him get the drawer open and then slammed it shut, trapping his hand. Lopez drove a thin-bladed knife up between his ribs and held it there till the blood had begun to seep between the banker's clenched teeth.

By the time the woman clerk had got her spectacles adjusted, some of the gang were starting to clear the drawers of money. The youngster wanted to make a move towards the pistol that was at the bottom of the filing cabinet down by his right hand but sheer terror prevented him from doing any such thing. Which was as well, for it probably prevented him from getting killed. As it was, the worst that happened to him was that he pissed himself and had to stand there with a dark patch widening and widening at the front of his best pants and a spreading pool of warm liquid on the floor between his polished boots.

The solitary customer wasn't so fortunate. A rancher who'd ridden the best part of a day into town to bank nigh on three hundred dollars, he didn't take any too well to watching a bunch of desperadoes take it out almost as soon as he'd passed it over the counter.

He waited until most of the gang were

eagerly scooping up money from the drawers or trying to persuade the terrified young clerk that if he didn't tell them how to open the safe they'd cut his *cojones* off and get him to eat them fried with a little chili sauce.

None of the men had bothered to search him for a weapon and he had an old Colt Navy loaded and tucked down into the front of his pants, the butt just above the belt. He took his time and got his hand inside his wool coat, waiting for the crash of a drawer on the ground before he pulled the gun clear.

He called a warning and cut loose on the first of the gang to try and draw. His shot struck the outlaw high in the chest and drove him back against the wall but it was the only shot he got to make. A volley of gunfire lifted him clear off the floor and deposited him in a bleeding, moaning heap close to the door. He had five slugs inside his body, three low in the guts, and two more had passed through him, one of them making a hole in his neck the size and shape of a second mouth.

It was going to take the rancher a long time to die; a long time in which to reflect painfully on the injustices of life in general and the banking business in particular.

Jake McCoy finished emptying the safe and called for his men to hit the street. As soon as the door swung open the front of the bank was raked with rifle fire from eight different positions along the far side of the street. The good citizens of San Pietro had not been wasting their time.

Jake ducked back inside and yelled for Nevada to take a couple of men and break out through the rear window and work a way round so as to give covering fire.

After a couple of minutes he ordered two of the bunch to bust through the front and make a dash for the mounts. No one seemed any too keen on that particular chore until Jake started flourishing his pistols in their direction. One of the breeds and a Mexican finally decided that they'd sooner take their chances out in the street than have Jake put a shell neatly in their brain pan.

The Mex didn't get off the boardwalk alive but the second man managed to free a couple of the broncs and swing himself half-way into the saddle of one of them before a lucky Winchester shell picked off his stetson and the back of his skull neat as you please.

By this time Nevada was blasting away from alongside the building and keeping the townsfolk pretty well pinned down. Jake led the bulk of the gang out through the front and they got on to their mounts without picking up more than a couple of flesh wounds and dropping one of the sacks of money.

Inside a brace of minutes they were galloping hell for leather down the main street, shooting out windows and sending bystanders flat to the ground in a desperate attempt to hang on to their lives.

McCoy's bunch lost three men and gained something in excess of one thousand dollars: all in all Jake McCoy thought the day's banking had shown a sight more profit than loss.

Less than three clear days after the bank robbery Jake McCoy, Nevada, Lopez and a string bean of a gunslinger who went by the name of Cotton Joe were in the general store in High Creek picking up supplies.

While they were waiting for the list of things to be made up Nevada teased Cotton Joe about buying half a dozen sticks of candy and Lopez wasted his time making eyes at the storekeeper's fifty-year-old wife. The horse-play between Nevada and Joe got to the point where Nevada almost made a play for his gun and the storeman's suspicions about his customers were prodded that bit harder.

While he was supposedly out back measuring out black-eyed peas into a three pound sack, he scribbled out a note to the sheriff and eased open the rear door awful careful. Charley Feathers was out in the alley again, sleeping off the previous night's drunk and hoping there'd be a few errands for him to run so's he could earn enough money to get drunk again.

He was soon running, hollow-legged, towards the sheriff's office.

"How much longer you goin' to be fiddlin' around back there?" called Jake.

"That about does it," said the store keeper. "There's just your coffee an' molasses and you're all set to go."

"Well, just see you ain't too damn long!" Jake moaned and sat down on a barrel of pickled fish.

The couple ground the beans slow and careful then poured the molasses through a narrow funnel into the jar Jake would stack with his other supplies. They had a flat-bed wagon out front, along with their mounts. The gang was fixing to stay in a couple of deserted shacks seven or eight miles from town, living off the fat of the bank raid and waiting until something else caught their fancy. Besides, they'd been running almost too many close calls with the law the past month or so and taking a while out of sight wouldn't do any harm. They sure didn't want no posse of United States deputies hunting them down and no Pinkertons neither. That would only mean they'd have to ride south of the Rio Grande again, and McCoy couldn't stomach *frijoles* and *tacos* as a steady diet if it could be avoided.

There soon wasn't anything the storekeeper and his wife could do to hang things out without McCoy getting suspicious. They totted up the price of the goods and Jake handed over the money grudgingly enough. He was turned towards the door, packages filling both arms when the door swung smartly open and he was staring into the sawed-off Remington of the sheriff.

Nevada let the sacks of flour drop to the floor and made a move for his Colt but the deputy backing up the sheriff covered his move with a Winchester and Nevada had the sense not to go through with his draw.

"What's the trouble, sheriff?" asked McCoy, keeping his voice as level as possible.

"Maybe nothin," replied the lawman, nudging the Remington closer to McCoy's belly.

"Then how come all the guns?"

"Had a rider through a day or so back. Seems there was a bank robbery over at San Pietro. Bunch of men got clear with a thousand dollars or so and rode out this direction." He stared into McCoy's face. "Feller bossin' the outfit, he was answerin' to your description I'd say. Two gun with fancy grips, tall, skinny and mean."

"That could be a lot of men," said McCoy.

The sheriff nodded. "Yeah. An' it could be you."

"What you figurin' on doin', sheriff?" asked Nevada.

"Gettin you boys down to the jail. Goin' through a bunch of fliers I got down there. See if you match up with any of 'em."

"An' if we don't?" asked Cotton Joe.

The lawman half-smiled, shrugged. "Then you're free to go on your way."

"Fine," said McCoy, taking a pace closer to the shotgun. "Let's go get it over with. No use standin' round here."

The sheriff stepped back to let McCoy pass in front of him. He swung the Remington almost into the small of his back and let the deputy cover the other three. McCoy was through the door and out onto the boardwalk before he made any kind of a move. The parcels were still in his arms and resting against his chest. Abruptly, he swung round and slammed his load down against the double barrels of the gun, leaping sideways at the same time. The Remington roared and blasted a sizeable chunk out of the floor of the empty wagon. McCoy's right hand dived for his pistol and as it swung up in a smooth arc, his thumb was bringing the hammer back.

The sheriff dropped into a crouch and let

the sawed-off fall, making a play for the Colt
Peacemaker at his own hip.

He didn't do bad.

His gun cleared leather and he almost got
it level before a slug hammered into his chest
close above the heart and sent him stum-
bling back against the storefront.

He pitched forward and a gush of blood
sped from his open mouth onto the ground.
His knees gave way and he smashed against
the boards with nothing to break his fall. If
he hadn't been already dead, the pain from
his broken nose would have been excruciating.

Meanwhile Nevada had dived to his left as
soon as he got through the door. Cotton Joe
had taken his cue and jumped the other way,
leaving the deputy a choice of targets. Lopez
sprinted forward and vaulted on to the back
of the nearest bronc. As soon as he hit the
saddle a bullet from the deputy's Winchester
drove into the animal's hind-quarters and
sent him sliding sideways to the dirt, pitching Lopez forward.

Nevada made his draw a few seconds ahead
of Joe and his .45 slug took the deputy in one
side the same time Joe's planted a .44 in the
other. Either way, the man was mortally
wounded and due to bleed to death inside
the next couple of hours.

Jake McCoy kicked open the store door

and backed the storeman and his wife against the wall while he took back the money he'd paid from the till—that and everything else that was there. He went to the door and then had second thoughts. Stepping smartly back, he pistol whipped the man for informing the sheriff and kneed the woman hard enough in the stomach to make her faint away. Then, with Lopez driving the wagon, they whipped up the horses and finally got their supplies out of town.

Blood on the High Creek boardwalk was all the payment they left behind.

Chapter Six

Cuchillo elbowed his way through coarse grass that stood stirrup high. Blue flowers, their heads round and tightly packed, were the sole interruption to the seemingly endless shades of green. The sides of the valley were steep and the creek that meandered along the bottom kept up a constant, almost metallic trickle as it splashed over rounded stones.

The two shacks were at the western end of the valley, one of them built on to the hill, the other at right angles to it and free-standing. The space between them had been fenced off as a corral and right now there were a dozen horses inside. Smoke drifted from a hole in the roof of the nearest shack. Out front of the other a man sat on a broken-backed chair, repairing the sole of his boot.

A second man was sitting on the corral fence, tending to a length of harness. The third, a Mexican, was digging a deep pit at the rear of the first shack, probably to bury excrement.

A bunch of men like these, there had to be a lot of shit!

Cuchillo had been watching the place for several hours and now he was trying to ease himself as close as he could; he still couldn't be certain how many men there were inside the two buildings. At various times, he'd spotted six but he was certain there were more. Just after he'd arrived, the one who looked like their leader—the one who wore two guns at his hips—had greeted a couple of riders who looked to have been travelling quite a ways. It seemed the gang was staging a rendezvous—could be it was social, could be some big job was being planned and they needed extra guns.

The Mexican lifted his shovel high and stuck the blade several inches into the earth. Then he arched his back as if feeling the effort of his work, twisted his head from side to side, and wandered off in search of a drink.

While he was scooping water from the barrel in front of the first shack, the boss man came out and exchanged a few words.

Cuchillo saw the Mexican shake his head

from side to side and the next moment the laughter of both men rose and echoed along the valley, gradually fading.

Cuchillo rolled on to his side and checked the position of the sun. It was time to move—he'd arranged to meet Marty three hours past noon and he didn't want the kid panicking and taking matters into his own hands.

He frowned, knowing that the boy was going to ask him one question only and not knowing the answer. He had no idea if the girl was in the shack or not. He didn't even know how many men were there. If he stayed where he was for three days he might never know.

If the girl was there, though, she was being kept awful quiet.

Cuchillo's eyes drifted back to the hole in the ground: maybe it wasn't intended for what he'd first thought. Maybe they had other plans—it didn't exactly look like a grave, but that didn't mean to say it couldn't be used as one. . . .

Cuchillo used his elbows and toes to move back through the swatch of grass to where his horse was hobbled over the ridge of the hill.

Marty was waiting impatiently by the dead remnants of the previous night's camp fire.

When the Apache rode in, the boy was covering him with a pistol held out front of his chest and gripped tight in both hands.

Cuchillo smiled: "It is good."

Marty ignored him. "Is she there? Did you see her?"

Cuchillo took his time dismounting, led the gelding over to a tree and looped the reins around a convenient branch.

"Damn it! Tell me!"

Cuchillo's face was impassive. "You could have built fire. Coffee would have been good."

"Did you see Natalie?" Marty's voice was close to a scream.

"No."

"No!"

He shook his head, squatted on his haunches. "The men are there, six or more. I saw no girl."

"Then Jesus Christ, what are we doin' here?"

"I did not say she was not there. Only I did not see her."

Marty shook his head violently. The pistol was still in his hand and it swung heavily as he waved his arms in frustration.

"Put down the gun," said Cuchillo.

"Put it down! I'll empty it into them bastards and make 'em tell me where the hell she is!"

He broke off abruptly, realizing that the answer they might give him were he able to do as he wished would not be the one he wanted to hear. He was fighting against the realization that she might be dead. They could have had their fill of her and she could be dead. Why would they keep her alive anyway when all she would be was a hindrance?

The expression on his face showed only too clearly what he was thinking.

Cuchillo looked at the boy and then at the flat, burning blue of the sky. "Cuchillo says, man who looks for death will find death, he who looks for life will find life."

Marty kicked his heel into the ground and dirt spurted over the ashes of the fire. "That's just talk! Indian talk! It don't prove nothin!"

Cuchillo shrugged, knowing that he had to let the boy calm down in his own time. He stood and busied himself with the gelding and the mare, making things to do. After a time, he asked, "What did you find out over in town?"

"Plenty. They were there right enough. Not too many days back. Sheriff an' one of his men tried to take 'em and got dead an' buried for their pains. That's what I found out."

"Nothing more?"

"Sure, more. Plenty more." Marty's face was flushed with excitement. "Feller runnin' the bunch is Jake McCoy. He took the bank in a town called San Pietro about a week back. Shot the place up pretty bad. When he was over in High Creek there weren't but him an' three others. They'd taken a wagon in for supplies. Sheriff, he come on 'em with a sawed-off or somesuch, had the drop on 'em an' everythin' and still they fought their way out." Marty spat on to the ground. "Bastards!"

Cuchillo nodded. "They are killers. Mean and vicious like wild dogs."

"An' they got Natalie."

"We don't know that. We only know they had her."

Marty stared at him with anger brimming into tears. "Don't you say that! Don't you ever say that!"

Cuchillo turned away. He knew that not giving voice to the thought wouldn't stop him thinking it—just as it wouldn't blank the thought from the boy's mind either. Everything suggested that the girl was dead by this time. Everything. But the only way Marty would give up his quest was if he found out for sure. And that meant one way or another they had to find out exactly who was inside McCoy's hide-out.

Cuchillo knew the problem—what he didn't yet know was a way of solving it.

*   *   *

It was dark save for a scattering of stars. The orange light smouldered under the logs of the fire and the sickly-sweet smell of young jack-rabbit hung on the air. A pan of strong black coffee bubbled lightly. Cuchillo sat licking the juice and grease from the ends of his fingers, working methodically, one by one. Marty was restless, fidgety. He reached for the pan and burned his fingers on the handle, cursed aloud and an owl returned his call from a nearby tree.

"We ridin' in there at sun-up, ain't we?"

Cuchillo looked at his shadow through the darkness; the flicker of small flames cast quick, agile shadows across his young face and made it suddenly old, a death mask that seemed to grin back at Cuchillo grotesquely.

The Apache felt a deep chill along his spine.

"Ain't we?" the boy persisted.

"No."

"What the hell . . . ?"

"We ride in there we'll be dead before we get close enough to call the girl's name."

"We can't wait here while. . . ."

"While they kill her?"

Marty's head spun with confusion. "What then?"

"We wait. Watch. Someone will leave. Then

we take him. He will tell us what we want to know."

Marty came around the fire, his hands bunched into fists and ready at his sides. "Damn you! Every minute we hang off, Natalie's in danger. Can't you understand that?"

Cuchillo shook his head. "If they want to kill girl, she is already dead. If they keep her alive, there is reason. She alive now, she stay alive. Nothing we do will change that—unless we ride in, attack. Then they kill her, sure."

"I don't understand what you're sayin'. What kinda reason they got for not . . .?"

Cuchillo gestured outwards with both hands. "Cuchillo not know reason. Only if they let her live there must be reason." He looked keenly at the boy. "Why they keep her alive?"

Marty shrugged and turned away. "I don't know," he mumbled.

Cuchillo watched the boy's face in the shifting light from the fire. He knew there was more going on inside the youth's troubled brain than he was telling.

In that, as in so many things, the Apache was right. Marty was indeed thinking of a reason why Jake McCoy might be keeping the girl alive—only for now he was keeping it to himself.

He stared blankly back at the Apache and slowly lifted the blanket around his shoulders. Both Cuchillo and the boy gazed into the fire and the noises of the night rose and fell about them; clouds scidded over the waning moon. Marty was lost in his thoughts of Natalie; Cuchillo in memories of his wife and child. When the wind bit into their bodies, they lay on either side of the fire and sought sleep.

One final hoot of the owl and everything was still. The clouds slid back across the moon and a sliver of pale light showed in the sky like a partly closed eye.

Cotton Joe tightened the cinch on the harness and patted the bronc on its broad, warm nose. He slid the Winchester up out of the scabbard and checked the action, made sure there was a shell ready to work into the breech. He put the looped thong of the water canteen over the curve of the saddle pommel and slotted his left boot into the stirrup.

"Joe!"

He cursed under his breath, swinging his head at McCoy's voice.

"You sure you got it clear?"

"Yeah, we went over it a dozen times."

"Okay, but it's important." McCoy laughed. "Five thousand dollars worth important."

Joe nodded. "Sure. If it works."

"It'll work."

Joe shrugged. He wasn't sure. He figured no man was going to shell out that much money for a kid who's been dragged around half of the state by a bunch of outlaws and the Lord knew what else. But Jake had got the idea fixed in his head and when he was like that you couldn't shake it clear any more than you could get the burrs out of the coat of a long-haired dog.

"You got the note?"

Joe patted his pants pocket.

"You ride in an' out. No risks."

"Don't worry."

Joe slid his boot back into the stirrup and pulled himself into the saddle. He slipped the small thong over the hammer of his Colt so that it wouldn't get shaken loose as he rode. The horse shifted impatiently under him.

McCoy stepped back. "See you in three days."

'Yeah.' Cotton Joe touched his fingers to the underside of his stetson, simultaneously touched his spurs to the animal's flanks. With a toss of the head, it broke into a trot.

Jake McCoy stood alongside the corral fence and watched him go, watched him all the way along the valley until he was little more than a shifting blur beside the creek. All the way he was counting the ransom money inside his head. One, two, three, four, five thousand.

A greedy smile lit his face when he eventually turned on his heel and strode back to the shack.

Marty licked his lips with a quick nervous gesture, the tip of his tongue flicking out like a lizard's. He was only too conscious of the sweat forming into a damp patch at the palm of both hands, the hollow pull of his guts. He gulped down a breath and it tasted raw. His eyes narrowed. He could see the man's head and shoulders now—he'd been able to pick up the steady pace of his mount's hoofbeats for the past mile.

The boy wiped the center of his right hand down the side of his pants and wished to God he had a gun at his belt.

"No gun," the Apache had said. "No gun."

And then: "You not afraid?"

He hadn't been about to admit to some Indian that he was afraid.

The man's face was clear as day. Marty told his stomach to stop rumbling. He touched his tongue once again to his dry lips and stepped quickly out.

"Mister!"

Cotton Joe whirled in the saddle, his right

hand letting the reins fall and flying to the
butt of his Colt.

"Hey, mister! Hold up a minute!"

Cotton Joe flicked the safety thing clear of
the Colt's hammer. He caught up the reins
with his left hand and brought the bronc to a
standstill some ten yards away from where
the boy was standing at the side of the trail.

"My horse went lame half a mile back."
Marty swung his arm and pointed down
through the pines. "Guess I never should've
gone off the trail."

Cotton Joe could see the kid had no weapon; he scanned the trees for signs of danger
but there weren't none. The youngster looked
straight enough.

"What you want me to do 'bout it?"

"I can't as much as lift him over, get my
saddle off him. Not on my own I can't."

Joe thought about it. McCoy was wanting
him to get where he was going in an all-fired
hurry but then Jake McCoy always wanted
things done that way. He shrugged. Maybe
this time he was going to have to wait five
mintues. It sure wouldn't hurt him none.

"You want to jump up behind?"

Marty's face broke into a smile. "Thanks,
mister!"

Joe shifted the horse forward and reached

down a hand, pulling the boy up and swinging him round behind the saddle.

"Where you say this was?"

"Down there through the trees. Ain't more'n half a mile."

"Okay. Let's go."

He touched his spurs to the animal's sides and ducked his head under the branches, keeping low until they had passed through the first twenty yards and the pines thinned out.

Joe half-turned. "What was you doin' down here anyway?"

When he didn't get an answer he turned back round and saw Cuchillo. The Apache was standing between two thick-trunked trees, arms folded across his chest.

"What the fuck!" yelled Joe and went for his gun.

It wasn't there.

A second later he felt the unmistakeable coldness of the barrel end pressing hard against the nape of his neck. He heard the triple click as the hammer came slowly back. His blood froze.

The Apache's arms were no longer folded and he, too, had a pistol covering him.

Cotton Joe's throat was dry and he cursed himself for being suckered that way by an Indian and a kid. Now he was going to lose his gun and the money he had in his pants pocket; he was going to say goodbye to two saddle bags crammed with supplies and likely his horse as well. He pictured Jake's face when he'd finally trudged back to the camp and explained how he'd lost his mount.

"Get down!" said Cuchillo.

"Down!" echoed Marty and vaulted to the ground.

Joe did as he was told, careful not to give either of them an excuse to shoot. If he was going to get robbed there wasn't much point in stopping a couple of slugs in the process.

It was only when they tied him to the nearest tree and the Apache produced the knife from behind his back that Cotton Joe slowly began to understand that it wasn't his horse and money they were after at all.

Half an hour later, Cuchillo leaned down and wiped the triangular blade on the unconscious man's pants. Marty read the note perhaps for the twentieth time. Neither his reading nor Cuchillo's was very good and he was sorely grieved to discover that Hedges' teaching of the Apache had been as good as he'd learned from his mother.

"You say parents dead," said Cuchillo sharply.

Marty shrugged and looked away.

"If dead, why this? Why. . . ." He fumbled for the right word.

"Ransom," Marty obliged for him.

"Why ransom if parents dead?"

Marty didn't look at Cuchillo as he spoke. "Okay, so they ain't dead. So what? They kept her locked up, that's what they did. Wouldn't let her out, talk to other kids, nothing."

"You steal her," Cuchillo accused.

"Hell! I didn't steal her. We run away together, that's all."

"You run. To California. You live on farm."

"No." Marty shook his head angrily. "We do that, he'll come looking for her sooner or later. Her father. We're gonna get on a boat, go somewhere no one'll ever find us."

"Maybe," said Cuchillo, "but we must find girl first."

"Yeah, an' now we know exactly where she is."

Cuchillo nodded, the boy was right. The only thing they had to figure out now was how the hell they were going to get her out.

Chapter Seven

Nevada kicked the door open and lurched against the wall. His eyes were bleary and red and he had a two-day stubble on his face. His shirt was unbuttoned and an almost empty bottle of rotgut whiskey dangled from his left hand.

Natalie was on the bunk bed low on the right side wall. She saw him and instinctively huddled back as far as she could, scrabbling the covers up to her chin. Her eyes were wide and staring, her face pale and drained. Her expression read of pain—pain and the expectation of pain. Until McCoy's bunch had taken her she had had no imagination of what a female body could endure and still live. There had been so many times when she had wished, prayed, that she was not alive. But death had taunted her and refused to come near.

Nevada came near.

The two men left on guard got up from the table where they'd been playing blackjack and moved to intercept him.

"Get out of here!" Nevada's voice was rasping and high.

"You get out, Nevada," answered one of the men.

A sneer slid across his face and the pistol was out of his holster and tight in his hand faster than any man that far in liquor should have been capable of.

"Don't you tell me what to do!"

"It ain't us." They both backed off a little, spreading left and right. "It ain't us, it's Jake. You know he says she's got to be left alone."

Nevada laughed. "Yeah, 'cept for him. He reckons she's all his now, don't he? Well, he can think what he likes, I'm takin' what I want when I want it."

"Nevada, why don't . . .?"

The gun barrel jerked sideways and up. "Why don't you do like I said and get the fuck out of here!"

The two men glanced at one another. They'd seen Nevada times enough when he was drunk and knew he was even less predictable than when sober—and then he was bad enough. Jake had given them their orders but maybe that didn't include getting shot. They looked at the girl hopelessly and headed for the door.

Nevada swung after them. "You keep your mouths shut. Anyone comes rushin' in here, I'll take care of them and after that I'll come after the pair of you. You understand that?"

They nodded: they understood. They went out and left Nevada and the girl together.

Nevada smiled lop-sidedly. He slotted the pistol back into his holster and lifted the bottle to his mouth, tilting back his head. The raw liquor ran down both sides of his mouth as he gulped and swallowed too fast. He jerked the bottle away and coughed till his eyes began to water, wiping his sleeve back and forth across his mouth.

Natalie watched him, only her eyes moving.

"Okay, girlie! Let's you and I play a little!"

Nevada went unevenly towards the bunk, almost falling at one point and pushing his hand against the wall to steady himself.

He reached towards her and she screamed.

He slapped the back of his hand across her face, his knuckles drawing blood from the corner of her mouth.

Natalie's eyes shone like pale fire, her nostrils flared.

"You little bitch!"

He ducked under the top bunk and grabbed

at her. Natalie waited till his fingers were
upon her face and opened her mouth fast,
biting down upon his middle finger hard.

Nevada yelled and jerked back, hammering his head against the wooden frame of the
bunk. Natalie was on him instantly, throwing back the covers and flailing her fingers at
his face. Her nails drew raking patterns down
his cheeks, blood seeping through almost at
once.

Nevada swung the bottle towards her head,
but his aim was poor and all that he succeeded in doing was smashing it against the
wall behind her.

"Fuck you, girlie! You're goin' to regret
this!"

He knocked her hands away from his face
and punched her on the side of the jaw.
Natalie was driven back against the wall, her
face singing with pain. She hadn't realized
that a single punch could hurt so bad. He
grabbed her shoulders at the second attempt
and lifted her bodily from the bunk, hurling
her across the room.

Natalie collided with the table and swung
round; she tried to keep her balance but it
was no good. Her legs skidded from underneath her and she stretched across the floor,
rolling into a chair and sending it flying. As

soon as she began to recover her breath, Nevada was on her.

His hand seized the collar of the torn, stained dress she was wearing and tried to tear it from her body. The stitches held, but only just. Natalie was dragged across the floor and Nevada shouted in exasperation. He aimed a kick at her side and she managed to evade it, rolling away and scrambling to her feet in the corner.

Spittle hung from the side of Nevada's mouth. "This time, girlie! This fuckin' time!"

He was almost upon her when the door to the shack swung open fast enough to crack one of the planks as it hammered back against the wall.

"Hold it, Nevada!"

He recognized Jake McCoy's voice even as he turned. He knew that McCoy would be angry enough to make this cause for a showdown. He faked a shambling turn to the left and then spun on his heel to the right, his brain suddenly slapped sober by the danger of the moment. If he'd made a fast draw before when he was facing up to the guards, he was quicker than hell now.

It didn't matter.

McCoy had come into the place with his Colts drawn and cocked and level. He waited while Nevada went through his double-shuffle and put a slug through his chest, not more than an inch above the heart. He grinned as the outlaw was hurled backwards and angled the left-hand gun to cover him. He thought about all the times when Nevada had been drunk and loud-mouthing, telling him that no man could use two guns as well as they could one. McCoy squeezed back on the trigger with the forefinger of his left hand and shot Nevada an inch below the first wound.

Nevada bucked forward and his heart burst.

His body hemorrhaged heavily.

Blood vomited from his mouth, dribbled from his nostrils and his ears.

He slapped hard against the cold floor.

Jake McCoy laughed.

At that exact moment the first flaming arrow thudded into the door of the other shack. A couple of seconds later the second arrow flew through the uncovered window and embedded itself midway down the interior wall.

One of the McCoy's men rolled off the top bunk and ran, hollering, for the door. Cuchillo set down his makeshift bow and steadied the pistol against the forearm of his other hand. As the man came running out, Cuchillo shot him through the thigh, close to his hip. It hadn't been his precise intention to shoot him there, any more than he'd meant for his first arrow to hit the door, but both had pretty much the desired effect.

McCoy came back out of the further back of the two shacks at a run, the rest of the bunch with him—that left the dead and still bleeding Nevada and the girl alone inside.

Cuchillo smiled with his eyes and kept the rest of his body still; he didn't want to spoil his aim. Still smiling, he squeezed back on the trigger. Dirt spurted up a few inches alongside McCoy and the outlaw boss jumped back and dived for cover alongside the shack.

Flames were beginning to climb the inside wall now, and smoke, dark and thick, was billowing through the nearest window. The bedding had caught fire and was burning fast.

Cuchillo had not got as close as he would have liked—his kind of shooting with a handgun wanted closer range than that—but the side of the valley didn't present him with any closer cover. As it was he was jammed down into a narrow crevice which threatened to hold him trapped.

McCoy was shouting orders but the attackers still had surprise working for them and as long as Cuchillo could keep them believ-

ing they were under fire from more than one,
they stood a chance of carrying out their
plan.

The Apache loosed off another arrow and,
almost immediately, followed it up with a
couple of snap shots from the Colt.

Inside the rear building, Natalie gingerly
set her hands against Nevada's body and
pushed as hard as she could. He shifted along
the floor with a slow, sucking sound and a
line of blood bubbles appeared between his
ribs and the floor.

Natalie grunted and caught her breath: she
gritted her teeth together and looked away,
heaving the dead man over onto his side. He
wobbled there for a moment and then slowly
collapsed back again—it was long enough for
the girl's small, slender fingers to snatch the
gun.

She knelt up and grasped it tight, using
both thumbs to click back the hammer.

The sound of the hammer was joined by
that of a footfall at the door.

Natalie spun round, swinging the long-
barrelled gun with her.

She gasped and her mouth stayed open.

Marty held a finger against the middle of
his lips, signalling for quiet.

He glanced around the room. Outside there

was still the sound of shouting and gunfire, the crackle of burning wood.

"Come on!" he mouthed.

She knew enough to release the hammer carefully before she obeyed. Running across the room towards him, she saw that he was staring at the marks on her face with a mixture of sorrow and anger. She blinked and shook her head as if to say that doesn't matter now.

Marty grabbed at her wrist and pulled her through the door and quickly to the rear, where the wall was a tumble of earth. They began climbing, not bothering about noise, hoping the sound of their escape would be covered in the commotion caused by the Apache's attack. They scrambled on hands, knees and feet, fifty feet to go before they could drop down into a broad ravine and find the two horses.

Cuchillo saw them on the slope and pushed cartridges down into the chamber of the Colt. A rifle slug drove into the hard earth less than twelve inches from his right shoulder and he blinked his eyes closed as dirt sprayed over him. One of McCoy's bunch was running towards him, while the others gave him covering fire. Cuchillo tried to get his head up enough to take aim, but more dirt needled into his face and he ducked back down again.

The Mexican was no more than twenty yards away when Cuchillo finally got his shot in. It didn't drop him right off, but the way the slug burrowed through the side of his calf made running kind of hard. He hopped some five yards more before falling to his knees and starting to crawl.

Only now he wasn't looking for Cuchillo, he was looking for cover.

He nearly found it.

Cuchillo dropped the Mexican face-down in the dust and saw Marty and the girl disappearing from sight as they dropped into the ravine. At much about the same time, McCoy realized the girl had been left on her own. He raised a holler and sent men scuttling back to the shack. The fire in the first place was smouldering to nothing.

Cuchillo put another couple of slugs between the bunch and himself and hightailed it back to his own mount as fast as he could. Half a mile along the valley rim he met up with Marty and the girl. It didn't take more than a few seconds to see what sort of a time she been put through. He read the concern and hatred on the boy's face, the relief and pain on the girl's.

She had looked frightened when the tall Apache had first come towards them, but Marty had spoken to her quickly, convincing her that it was all right.

Cuchillo immediately took the lead and led the couple west towards the tree line.

After riding the best part of four hours without let-up, they found refuge in a small deserted mission building on a low hill to the north of the trail. Little more than the adobe shell remained, a place that had been built to serve some small community that had long since moved on.

There was a well in the center of the courtyard and the wheel that worked the bucket pulley was creaky and complaining, but worked nonetheless.

"We got to build a fire," said Marty. It was almost the first thing he'd said to Cuchillo since they'd made the escape.

The Apache shook his head.

"We must!"

"You don't think they will be following us? The girl, she is worth much money to them. They will not simply allow us to take her."

Cuchillo glanced over his shoulder towards the edge of the courtyard, as if expecting men to ride through the entrance at any moment.

"You can see the state she's in," said Marty, lowering his voice. "She's got to be kept warm. She ought to have hot water to wash, somethin' hot to drink."

"Being clean will not help her if the smoke from the fire brings them back to us."

Marty shook his head stubbornly. "We don't have that choice. An' it's too late to go on now. It's gettin' dark and the horses are just about spent."

Cuchillo knew that that was true. And maybe the fact that they'd made such good time would keep McCoy and his men at their back till first light. He shrugged and folded his arms across his chest. "Make your fire."

Marty grinned and hurried away.

Cuchillo looked at the girl. When he and the boy had begun talking about the fire, he had thought she was asleep. Now she was staring at him, her eyes wide and wild. Cuchillo turned away and went towards the horses. There was something about her that unsettled him, something in her eyes that reminded him of the holy men of his tribe who went off into the wilderness on vision quests. It was the piercing intensity of the gaze, the fire, the pale fire. . . .

Cuchillo stopped in his tracks as a bird broke from the gnarled tree close to the mission entrance. He saw its dark shadow and heard the slow flapping of its wings as it circled overhead, looking for prey.

He knew they were out there, the only thing he didn't know was how close or how far.

When he went back into the courtyard, Marty had brought together enough wood to start a fire. The girl was sitting cross-legged and leaning against the rough adobe of the wall; her hands were crossed over her chest on to her shoulders and she was singing in a low, melodic voice—no words that Cuchillo could hear, just musical sounds like a bird's song.

The sadness of the song rose softly towards the darkening sky.

Marty set a blanket across her shoulders and she continued singing, almost as if she was no longer noticing anyone or anything around her.

"How 'bout the fire?" said Marty.

Cuchillo nodded. "Keep it small. We will keep watch. Leave before first light."

He left them huddled together around the orange glow and climbed as far as the clumsy

steps of the tower permitted. The top section
had crumbled away and he squatted with his
shoulders pressed against the edge, hands
resting on the pistol on his legs. If anyone
approached he would hear them and there
would be sufficient light to pick out their
shapes if they came close to the mission.

Cuchillo closed his eyes and concentrated
on the sounds around him. He brought into
the center of his mind a miscellany of night
sounds that had not seemed present moments
before. When he had placed them all, he
moved the concentration to his body—the
texture of the wall behind him and the floor
beneath him, the metal and wood of the pistol between his fingers, the movement of the
wind across his face.

He was so alive to his senses that he heard
the girl fall seconds before Marty, who had
been almost touching her.

Cuchillo sprang to his feet and ran, almost
soundlessly, down the steps of the tower.

Natalie had half-rolled, half-fallen across
the remains of the fire. The blanket she had
wrapped about herself was smouldering and
the skirt of her dress had begun to burn.

Marty came awake with a start and saw
what had happened. He was reaching for her
as Cuchillo ran hard across the courtyard.

The Apache seized her legs as the boy lifted her from beneath her arms and they hauled her clear of the fire and rolled her in the dirt. Marty slapped down at the thin cotton, flattening out the flames.

Cuchillo pulled the blanket from her and hurled it away.

Natalie sprang to her feet and her mouth opened in a howl that stopped them in their tracks. Her head was thrown back and her eyes clenched tight, her mouth was wide and calling at the moon.

Cuchillo jumped forward and put his hand over her mouth to still the sound.

She brought her teeth, small and sharp, down into the flesh at the base of his middle finger.

Cuchillo jerked his hand away, blood running into the palm of his hand. He clenched his fist and moved as if to strike her; Marty pushed himself between them, keeping the Apache at bay.

"Don't you touch her!"

Cuchillo let his hand relax, stepped back. Marty stood his ground. Behind the boy, Natalie was staring through the darkness at Cuchillo, the light of anger in her eyes strong enough to pierce the gloom.

"You want to kill me!" she shrieked.

Cuchillo shook his head.

Marty turned towards her, gently stretching out a hand. "That ain't true. He helped me get you away, don't you remember?"

The girl shook her head. She felt his fingers touch her and she lept back with a shudder.

"Natalie! What is it?"

She fell forward on to her knees and her whole body was racked with convulsions. She clutched at herself as if trying to stop the shaking, but it was no use. When Marty moved towards her, she screamed and made him back away.

Cuchillo ran to the mission entrance. If anyone had kept riding through the night in pursuit of them, they would certainly hear the girl and know where they were.

But there were no human sounds out there in the night. He waited for several moments, while behind him the girl's torment seemed to be calming. When he went back to them, Marty had quieted her and replaced the charred blanket about her shoulders. Natalie was staring into space, the fire of her eyes directed against something neither Cuchillo nor the boy could see.

"Is she all right?"

Marty looked up and nodded. "She'll be okay now. You don't have to worry none."

Cuchillo pointed at the girl. "Does she often. . . ."

"You know what she's been through!" Marty interrupted him. "She's bound to react some way, ain't she? S'only natural."

Cuchillo turned away, wondering just how natural the strange young girl really was.

Chapter Eight

Jake McCoy shook himself and buttoned the front of his wool pants. He hawked some bitter phlegm from the back of his throat and spat it on to the brilliant blue head of a wild flower. He hunched his shoulders and turned back towards the fire.

The other men were either standing or sitting around it, Bitter Moon leaning back against his saddle and rolling a cigarette. Juan stirred a mush of beans and jerky in a heavy-bottomed black pan. Coffee was bubbling a little too fiercely at the opposite side of the fire.

McCoy scooped a mug from the ground and poured himself a cup of coffee. He grimaced as he tasted the first mouthful, but drank it nevertheless. The early morning was cold as hell, even though by midday they

would all be bathed in sweat—men and an-
imals alike.

There were seven of them: McCoy himself,
Bitter Moon and a half-breed Comanche who
went by the name of Charlie Cloud, Juan and
Lopez, a bowlegged wrangler from up Wyo-
ming way called Lefty Burnette, and Skinny
Ennis, who was a long-time gunfighter with
a notched Colt Peacemaker and a left eye
made from colored glass.

McCoy knew it wasn't going to be easy
keeping them together for long, chasing across
California after some half-wild girl. Robbing
banks and holding up stages they could
understand—the money was there for their
taking and a man either took it or got himself
shot in the attempt. But going after some girl
because her father might shell out five thousand dollars some time in the future, that
was different.

Already there was grumbling coming from
one or two of them—Lefty and Skinny chewing away at it to themselves, Bitter Moon
living up to his name and getting in as much
bitching as he could.

Well, he shown them with Nevada what
he did if one of his bunch crossed him. If he
had to do it again, he would. Just as long as
they understood.

Juan spooned the breakfast out onto tin

plates and everyone ate without relish but from necessity, washing it down with more coffee and then hurrying to saddle up their broncs and get moving.

". . . wastin' our damn time chasin' after some. . . ."

Lefty didn't get any further. McCoy seized hold of his right arm above the elbow and stopped him in his tracks, swinging him round. Lefty's mouth opened in protest and as it did so McCoy's fist, clenched tight, hammered hard under his heart.

Breath sighed from Lefty's chest as he staggered back as far as McCoy's grip on him would allow.

His gun was holstered the side his name suggested and his left hand made a move to cover it in case McCoy decided to swing his fist a second time.

Maybe it wasn't going to be necessary.

McCoy didn't have much intention of throwing another punch. His hand was no longer clenched but the fingers were spread wide and held in a curve above the butt of his Colt.

"I reckoned I'd told you enough times," McCoy said. "All of you. There ain't but one person givin' the orders in this outfit an' that's me."

Lefty shook his head. "I never said anythin' different, Jake."

"You kept that mouth of yorn shut you wouldn't say anything at all."

Lopez laughed and Charlie Cloud cackled into the back of his hand in a passable imitation of a chicken.

Not Skinny Ennis—him and Lefty, they'd buddied up since starting to ride with McCoy and Skinny didn't take to seeing his friend pushed around that way. Especially by someone like McCoy who was getting too big for his boots by half. He needed taking down a step or two and Skinny figured he might be the man to do it.

Lefty wasn't sure. Not after the way McCoy had dealt with Nevada. He'd never figured Nevada to be a slouch with a gun, but Jake had killed him like he was taking shooting practice out by the back fence.

Now he glanced at Skinny and read the look in his one good eye and shook his head.

Jake McCoy saw the look and read it right and laughed.

"Lefty," he said with a grin, "you just stopped your friend there from gettin' hisself shot up before he's had time to digest his breakfast."

Skinny snorted and kicked his heels down into the dirt, but he didn't do anything more.

Lefty shrugged and said: "I ain't got no quarrel with what you say, Jake. We done pretty good ridin' for you an' that's the truth. It's just. . . ." He broke off and looked away.

"Just what?" asked McCoy threateningly.

"Some of the boys. . . ."

"Some?"

"Well, Skinny an' me. . . ."

"That's more like it."

"We been wonderin'. . . ."

"Spit it out!"

"How long we gonna ride after this girl an' whoever she got with her?"

Bitter Moon scuffed a couple of paces forward. "Yeah, boss. How long?"

"How long, Jake?" said Skinny.

Jake snorted and set both hands on to the grips of his .45s. "The whole bunch of you, huh? Don't trust me, huh? Lefty's right ain't he? Since any of you rode with me you had grub in your bellies and money in your pockets. You had women and liquor when you wanted 'em and there ain't none of you got taken by the law. What else d'you want?"

There was a silence that seemed to stretch a long time. And then, out of the quiet, Skinny's voice asking: "Do we ride after this fool girl till we catch up to her, no matter what?"

McCoy's eyes narrowed and his body dropped slightly, easily into a gunfighter's natural crouch. Both hands were on their guns.

"You sure believe in pressin' your luck, don't you? Specially for a man ain't got more'n one eye."

Skinny spat out of the corner of his mouth without ever shifting the position of his head or taking his eyes off McCoy. "Maybe one's all I need."

McCoy shook his head slowly from side to side. His eyes were narrower now and the fingers of his right hand had curled tight about the Colt's grip.

"We follow the girl till we catch her," McCoy said, "or till I say it's enough. You want to argue with that, you best make your move."

Skinny hesitated. He knew sure as all hell that there wasn't a thing that would give him more pleasure than leaving Jake in a pool of his own blood. But still the speed of McCoy's hands with those twin Colts of his put him off . . . and that hesitation was all it needed to keep him from making his move.

Instead he backed off and mumbled, "Okay, Jake. You're callin' the cards right enough."

The words almost choked in his throat, but he said them nonetheless. Lefty released his breath shakily, knowing that if his buddy had gone for his gun he would have had to do the same.

"Let's shake up!" called McCoy, turning away from the fire, showing the rest of the men that he didn't fear either Skinny or Lefty even when his back was towards them. "We got a lot of ridin' to do."

Cuchillo had been doing a deal of riding, too. Leaving Marty and the girl to travel at their own speed, he'd cut across country and hit the stage road that drove south towards the border. He knew there was a way station that would offer them hot food and a place to rest up; knew from Natalie's face that if she didn't get both, she wasn't going to make it much further.

As soon as they'd hit their saddles that day, she'd been leaning forward, face pale as the previous night's waning moon. After a couple of miles she reined in and slipped awkwardly to the ground, running ten yards off the trail before falling to her knees and vomiting, a thin trail of it hanging from her fingers to the hard ground.

Since then, she'd thrown up twice more, Marty standing anxiously over her each time, resting his hand on the back of her neck, as if willing her to get better.

Cuchillo didn't think the boy's wishes were

going to do a whole lot for her. He thought
rest and food might—but even then he wasn't
sure. He didn't even know if it was the treatment she'd received at the hands of McCoy's
bunch of outlaws that lay at the root of her
troubles; maybe it was something else, something deeper than that, something Marty had
kept silent about.

Cuchillo vowed to ask him as soon as he
got the chance.

That would have to wait.

Right now he was on the slope of grass
above the way station, making sure there were
no signs that McCoy's gang had crossed the
trail in front of them and got there first.

There were no more than six horses in the
corral and he guessed that four of those were
a fresh team for the next due stage. Likely
the other two belonged to whoever ran the
station. A couple of mules, one laden with
supplies, was tied up at the side of the main
building and there was a wagon with writing
on the canvas sides put up out front of the
barn. The barn itself stood at right angles to
the station and the corral was fenced out
from the rear of the barn.

Cuchillo knew it was a risk to bring the
girl here on account of it being the obvious
place to make a stop. From here the stage
road climbed north and west, gradually mak-

ing its way through the Salinas Valley and up towards San Francisco. That was where Marty wanted to take the girl. He intended to ship out to the Orient, the pair of them, away from the reach of Jake McCoy or the girl's family.

Cuchillo had seen San Franciso—he had nearly forfeited his life in Chinatown and he wasn't about to return. But if he could see the couple on their way, if he could get them clear of McCoy, then he'd have done what he could. Maybe it would help him to rest easier with the spirits of those close to him who came to trouble him in his rest.

Anyway, it had started and it must run its course to the end—whichever end that would be.

He swung his mount around and set off at a canter to where Marty and the girl would be making slow progress along the trail.

". . . fell off that ornery mule of his an' that ole Colt Navy pistol he always toted came spinnin' out of its holster and soon as it hit the ground it went off an' shot Omaha through the leg. Damned if that slug didn't ricochet off the bone an' slam into the rock, chippin' a hunk of the stuff clear away. When Omaha drags hisself to his hands and knees and quits moanin' 'bout how he ain't ever goin'

to be able to walk proper, he finds hisself
face to face with a vein of gold thicker'n
three fingers of your hand. Now ain't that the
damndest thing you ever heard?''

Clem Watson shifted his plug of chewing
tobacco from one side of his mouth to the
other and managed to spit a stream of almost-
black tobacco juice smack into the spitoon as
he did so.

He'd spent the last ten years of more of his
life listening to yarns like the one Doc
Murrayweather had just spun. He'd heard
'em in Yuba City and Marysville, Sierra City
and Grass Valley, Placerville and Lodi and
every mining camp small or large down the
mother lode. He'd heard how men had struck
it rich by chance and lost a fortune overnight
by bad luck each place he'd set down long
enough to listen: Jackson and Sonara and
Chinese Camp, Moccasin and Mariposa and
Second Garrote. Now he was working out his
days running a half-assed way station in the
middle of nowhere and they were still telling him the same old tales, like it was important to believe that if a man had the bad
fortune to fall off his horse and shoot himself
he'd have the good luck to find himself face
to face with a fortune at the same time.

The way Clem Watson saw life, that weren't
the way it was. Man fell off his horse and

shot himself he was like enough to end up dead. And if he only shot himself through the leg then the most likely thing was that gangrene would set in and he'd find himself on a scrubbed down table having the damned thing sawed off with nothing to help the pain but a hunk of wood to bite down on and a bottle of rotgut liquor to swallow and clean the bloody wound at the same time.

Clem reckoned that was closer to life than crawling on hands and knees till you was face to face with three fingers of gold.

He knew it wasn't any use saying so.

He nodded his head at Doc Murrayweather and allowed as how it was wonderful. Then he shuffled off towards the kitchen range, favoring his bad leg as he did so. There was a stew simmering away, ready for the passengers on the afternoon stage ... supposing there were any passengers ... supposing the stage made the trip.

Hell, none of that was his problem. There was a team ready to go, food ready to eat, a place for anyone who wanted to wash up and rest. He'd done his job well enough and no one in the company could say different.

"Got a beer?" called the old timer whose mules were stinking up the yard outside.

Clem nodded and hollered for the man to hang on. When he took the beer over to him,

he was careful not to get too close. The old
man claimed to have been in the hills for
nigh on three months and Clem believed him;
he also believed he hadn't taken a bath in all
that time, nor shaved, nor changed his clothes.
His long graying beard was dark around the
mouth with the constant dribbling of tobacco
and his patched and wrinkled skin was scal-
ing away from either side of his bulbous
nose.

"That stew ready soon?" the man asked.

"If you got the price for it," answered Clem.

"Sure have. Still got money in my pockets
from the strike I made up Folsom way back
in. . . ."

But Clem didn't want to hear two gold
rush stories one after the other. Him and
these two relics, that was what the gold rush
was about, they were what it came down to
when all the shouting and the ballyhoo were
over and done. A few big strikes and pretty
soon all the mines that were worth a damn
had been taken over by big companies with
enough money to pay to have them mined
proper. For the average prospector, it meant
little enough.

He glanced at the stinking old man, at the
fake doctor who eeked out a living peddling
patent medicines that were as likely to give
you pain as take it away. The two of them

and his crippled leg—that was California to Clem Watson.

He went slowly back to stirring the pan of stew, listening with half his mind for the grating rumble of stage wheels up along the track.

Natalie was leaning against a shelf of rock, her head resting on one arm, cold with beads of sweat. She had been retching for close to fifteen minutes, harsh hacking movements which had jerked her entire body forward and which seemed to be scraping the last remnants of her stomach painfully away.

When Marty had gone to stand with her she had thrust him away, told him to leave her be.

Finally the boy had obeyed, walked slowly back to where Cuchillo stood in the shade, patient and alert.

"She sick before this," the Apache said, careful that the girl should not hear him.

"Course she ain't. I told you before, it's what them stinkin' bastards done to her made her this way."

But the expression on Cuchillo's face made it clear that he did not believe the lie. Marty tried to avoid the accusation in the Apache's eyes but it was like wriggling at the end of a length of fishing line after the bait had been took.

"Natalie, she was . . .," he hesitated, talking low, not looking at Cuchillo as he spoke, ". . . she was sick from a little kid. Not just sick, I mean, they—her folks—they reckoned as how she was wrong in the head. Times she wouldn't speak to anyone for days on end. Other times, she would seem to go off into a trance and then . . . and then she would have fits. Nothing dangerous most of the time. She'd fall over and roll on her back and her mouth would . . . would froth and they'd have to push something between her teeth to stop her bitin' off her own tongue."

Marty glanced over at where Natalie was still leaning forward against the rock.

"They had doctors to her an' all sorts, but it never done any good. Most the time they let her run free but never without someone close to look after her. As she got older she got worse, fits'd start without warnin', her pa he took to lockin' her up whenever company come by." Marty wiped his sweating hands down the side of his pants. "They was fixin' to send her to some place back east, some hospital kind of place where they'd keep her locked up." He looked at Cuchillo. "Weren't no hospital, it was a madhouse. They never said that, not outright, but I knew that's what it was."

Cuchillo pointed. "And the girl? She knew also?"

Marty shook his head. "Who knows what Natalie understands? Sometimes I reckon she don't rightly understand what's goin' on around her . . . like what we're doin' now. Other times, seems to me she knows more'n the rest of us put together."

Cuchillo thought of the shamen of his tribe, whose fits and visions made them different from all others. They saw what ordinary men could never hope to see, understood what no one else could hope to understand until he became one with the spirits through death.

He set a hand on the boy's shoulder. "How will you be with her when you are alone?"

Marty wiped his forehead with the back of his hand. Natalie was vomiting again— straining to, the sound fierce and dreadful— and he was trying not to notice. "We'll be okay. She trusts me. When we're on board that ship it'll be different. She'll be better then, I know it."

He looked at the Apache earnestly, tears pricking against the backs of his eyes. "She'll be better. I know it. I do."

Cuchillo nodded, not believing it, yet wanting to for the boy's sake. For both their sakes. He checked the position of the sun in the sky.

"Come," he said quietly. "Go to her. We must ride."

The stage rattled and bounced its way north-wards, its three passengers toppling from side to side with each fresh lurch of the coach. They had all three been travelling for five days, north from the border. In another three days they would reach their destination. By then their throats would be dry as rough-cast rock from the dust and their bodies would be a mass of bruises from the rigors of the road.

As for Jim Mitten up on the driver's seat, he didn't give a two-cent damn for what was happening inside. All he cared about was getting this particular stage into Sacramento in one piece. He'd been making the same run for six years and he knew each and every bend in the road, each tree and outcrop of rock that showed along it. Now he was mak-ing his last journey.

The company would have kept him up there in the driver's seat for another six years or more, but that wasn't the way Jim saw it. He'd found himself a widow woman with a hankering to get married and a dining room and lodging house south of Sacramento that would keep the two of them just fine.

There'd be plenty of work for him to do without getting shaken so hard his bones were like to start chipping away bit by bit. He'd lived a hard enough life that a deal of comfort wouldn't come amiss. And he wouldn't any longer have to be keeping an eye out for bandits riding down out of the hills or suddenly turning up in front of him on the road. Nowadays the company didn't even bother with a shotgun guard unless they was carrying something special in the strong box. The passengers were all told that they were travelling at their own risk and if they were still fool enough to carry anything of value with them, well it weren't no one else's fault if they lost it.

Jim had a sawed-off down by his feet, right enough, but he didn't figure it was his job to reach for it and get shot to protect someone else's bill-fold or gold watch.

That weren't what he was being paid for.

If he saw a gang bearing down on him, he'd slow the team down and shift his hands into the air as soon as they got within range. That way he'd stayed alive and in one piece through seven hold-ups in the last three months alone.

Seven too many. He'd be damned pleased if he could make this last run without making it eight. One last clean drive and he'd turn in his whip and shotgun back where they belonged, draw his final pay check and ride back to where the widow was waiting patiently.

The front wheels bumped over a ridge in the road and inside the passengers were hurled into a heap, the whiskey drummer's case colliding with the woman's shoulder, the wine shipper's hat falling against the drummer's face. They picked themselves up and made their usual complaints, rescuing their belongings and sitting back against the sagging upholstery.

The drummer fingered his watch from the small pocket at the front of his vest and clicked it open. "We should have been at the station almost an hour since."

"If he keeps driving this stage the way he is," said the other man, "we'll be lucky to get there at all."

The woman shook her head. She was riding away from the funeral of her husband and son, both stricken with fever and dead within two days of one another. Her late husband had a sister who lived in San Franciso and she was hoping to join her there. If that didn't work out, she didn't know what she would do.

She looked through the window and the never-changing hills that had confronted her for days. If they were any different she never noticed. Right now she was living for that way station, a chance to wash-up, rest her aching limbs.

"Lucky if we get there at all," the man was repeating.

The whiskey drummer agreed.

"We'll get there all right," said the woman quietly, as much to convince herself and anything else. "We'll get there right enough."

Skinny Ennis loosened the cinch of his lathered bronc and let the animal push its head down to the water that sparkled in the creek.

Lefty moved in alongside him, his mount's reins loose over his glove.

"How long we goin' along with this, Skinny?" Lefty asked quietly, glancing round to make sure McCoy was out of earshot.

Skinny didn't look at him, carried on with what he was doing. "No longer'n we got to. First good chance we get, I'm breakin' out. We got us better things to do than go after some damn girl. I never reckoned her pa'd pay out that kind of money, anyhow."

"Me neither," agreed Lefty. "Only thing is, how 'bout Jake? He ain't exactly goin' to give us his blessin's."

Skinny Ennis blinked his good eye. "Don't you worry 'bout that bastard none. I'll settle for him—even if I have to wait till he's got his back turned!''

Jake McCoy moved towards them, and Lefty turned his horse away without another word. Skinny refastened the cinch and slotted his boot into the stirrup. Jake had said they were riding to the way station out on the north-bound trail and for now that was exactly what they were going to do—let him think things were going just the way he wanted them. He'd find out soon enough that they weren't.

Chapter Nine

Cuchillo rode in first, Marty and the girl some fifty yards behind. The same pair of mules were tethered at the side of the main building, the same wagon was by the barn. Harness was draped over the rails of the corral like someone was expecting to make a change of horses, but there was no sign of any stage.

Cuchillo dismounted and signalled for Marty to bring the girl in. As the boy was helping Natalie from the saddle, Clem Watson pushed aside the piece of sacking that hung down from the window and peered out. When he saw the youngsters, he didn't think a whole lot, apart from it'd be nice to see a female around the place for a change. But then he saw the tall Apache and he thought plenty.

Quickly, he limped back from the window and pulled open the utensils drawer back of the counter. In amongst the carving knives and can openers and such was an American Arms shotgun that he'd had with him for the best part of seven years. In all that time he'd only had cause to fire it twice, though he'd brandished it countless times. On the first occasion he'd put the weapon to use, he'd gut-shot a rustler who was appropriating a dozen head of company horses. The man's shirt and coat had been shredded into the front of his belly and blood and excrement had been sprayed for an area of maybe ten yards. The thief had moaned and cried for the best part of a couple of hours, begging all the while he was conscious for Clem to finish him off. But Clem reckoned he needed time to think on his wicked ways and repent so he left him to it.

The second time he used the gun was when a fight broke out in the way station and it looked as if a month's supplies was about to be destroyed as six or more drunken miners celebrated their pay by lashing out at everything in sight—including each other. Clem gave them three shouted warnings and even discharged a pistol into the ceiling. None of that appeared to have any effect.

When they put their boots through two of

his barrels of beer, Clem swung the shotgun high round his head and broke one man's jaw with the stock. He drove the end fast into a second miner's face and busted his nose in three places. It still wasn't enough to calm the rest—all it did was turn their attentions to him.

One came for him with a pistol, two pulled knives out of their belts and a fourth brandished the broken back of a chair. Clem showed them both barrels and assured them he meant business: either they didn't believe him or they were too drunk to care. The nearest man got close enough to cut a slice out of Clem's arm before he shook him aside and fired the contents of one barrel at the remaining three. O-O shot flew into faces and chests and necks and all of them got sobered up pretty damned fast. Clem slipped a fresh cartridge down into the empty barrel and followed them out to their horses, blood dripping all the way. He waited weeks for them to come back and take some kind of revenge, sleeping in an old rocker down by the stove, the shotgun across his knees and a candle burning. No one ever showed and gradually Clem forgot all about the affair.

Except that it did leave him a shade more cautious than before. Which was why he now had the gun on the top of the counter underneath a fading copy of a San Diego paper someone had brought in on the stage.

Doc Murrayweather looked up from where he'd been dozing close to the stove. "Trouble?"

Clem shook his head. "I ain't sure."

Across the room the old prospector hawked spit into his mouth, pushed it around some with his tongue and swallowed it back down.

The door opened and Cuchillo came inside.

"Jesus Christ!" hissed the doc.

Clem Watson let his fingers slide a shade higher up the stock of the gun.

The Apache looked a formidable sight. Simply by his size he was more than impressive—but with a pistol sticking up conspicuously from his belt and a hostile look on his face, he was a figure to induce both fear and respect.

Cuchillo looked round the room quickly, his eyes like those of a bird of prey. "Who else here?" he asked Clem Watson behind the counter.

"Ain't no one else."

"You not lie?"

"Search the place if'n you want."

Cuchillo nodded abruptly and called for Marty without turning his head. The boy brought Natalie through, one arm around her shoulders. She looked pale and almost lifeless, walking in hesitant steps as if sleep-

walking through a dream she failed to recognize.

When they were in the main room, Cuchillo
shut the door fast.

"You got a place where she can wash up?"
asked Marty, gesturing towards the girl.

"She sick?"

"She's okay," replied Marty a little too
fast.

Clem shifted his gaze from the youth to
the Apache and then over to the girl, who
was sitting now on the long bench beside the
dining table.

"How 'bout it?" asked Marty, impatient.

"Sure." Clem pointed past the counter to a
narrow door. "Through there. A couple of
cots in there if'n she needs to lie down."

"She's okay, I tell you. We just ridden a
long way, that's all."

Clem shrugged. "Suit yourself."

Marty helped Natalie to her feet and walked
with her across the room. Doc Murrayweather
swallowed down the last of his cheap whiskey and cleared his throat, getting off his
chair with as much dignity as he could
muster.

"I have to observe, young man," he began,
as Marty turned back from the door, "that
your companion is in some distress and sorely
in need of expert medical assistance. This

being the case, permit me to introduce my-
self. My name is. . . ."

"I don't give a hog's ass what your name
is, old man! You ain't got nothin' to say to
me and nothin' to give to her."

And Marty pushed past the doc and made
his way to where Cuchillo was standing between the main door and the stove.

"Young man," Murrayweather turned, trying
to recover face, "I'll have you know that I
have treated the famous and the wealthy in
this state for many more years than you have
been walking upon it. And it is my medical
advice to you that unless that young lady
receives treatment and care such as I am able
to give, she may not continue with you for
much longer on your journey."

Marty clenched his fists and went at the
doctor at a rush. He'd succeeded in landing
one punch at the side of Murrayweather's
jaw before Cuchillo grabbed him by the arm
and jerked him away. For a few seconds the
pair of them stood facing one another, Marty
breathing heavily, his fists still clenched tight
and ready to take a shot at the Apache's face.

"He was doing nothing," said Cuchillo.
"Meant no harm."

Marty controlled his breathing, slowly
began to relax his fingers.

"Could be he is right," Cuchillo went on, "medicine good for her."

"To hell with you!" shouted Marty in his face. "Ain't I told you, she don't need no patent medicines. All she needs is carin' for. That an' a ship away from this damned country! "There were tears close to falling as he spoke.

Cuchillo stood back and lowered his arms.

Doc Murrayweather stood whiping his chin, a thin sliver of pale blood trickling from the edge of his mouth.

Cuchillo turned towards the counter and said direct to Clem Watson's face. "You use gun or no?"

Clem pulled his mouth close together and tried to ignore the pain that was shooting up his bad leg—storms or other dangers, it let him know well in advance.

He shook the newspaper away from the gun. "Guess I'll use it if I have to."

"You not have to."

Natalie slowly opened the door from the back room and came out. She looked a shade better with the trail dirt washed from her face, but her skin seemed paler than ever, almost translucent. She looked at Cuchillo and then at Marty and she managed to give the boy a smile; it was almost the first sign of affection Cuchillo had noticed passing that was between them.

"You have food?" Cuchillo asked.

"Stew waitin' on the stage."

"She needs food now."

Clem pulled out his watch and checked the time. The stage was close to an hour late and the stew would be good and dried before anyone got the chance to eat it. He sighed and headed towards the stove. "How many of you hungry?"

"Three," Marty said quickly.

"Four," added the doc, making sure that he sat well away from the youngster on the long table.

"Five," said the prospector, "long as it ain't more'n fifty cents."

Clem spooned stew out onto cracked and chipped heavy china plates and carried them two at a time over to the table. He hacked slices from the cornbread loaf and passed these along, together with forks and knives. The food was dark and thick and some of the contents had started to shrivel, but at least it was hot and filling.

After her second mouthful, Natalie gagged and her hands flew to her mouth. She swung her legs around from the bench and hurried towards the back room, the men watching her go.

"I said as how. . ." Doc Murrayweather began, but stopped as soon as he saw Marty's face.

Even with the door closed they could hear the sounds of her retching, only gradually did any of them pick out the fresh sound of the stage making its final run-in to the station.

Skinny Ennis had joined the coach five miles short of its temporary destination. He'd positioned himself alongside the trail, saddle slung over his shoulder and saddle bags on the ground by his feet.

Jim Mitten hauled in on the reins and gradually applied the brake, bringing the stage to a bumpy halt. Ennis told some tale about his mount and assured Mitten he had enough money to pay for a ride to the way station, where he hoped to buy another mount.

The two men inside nodded a welcome, while the woman wrinkled up her nose at the smell of Skinny's trail dirt and sweat and the sight of his glass eye. Skinny didn't give a damn. He slung his saddle on top and sat inside next to the woman, exchanging words with the whiskey drummer and noticing that the proximity of the woman had a warmth to it he hadn't felt for so long he'd more or less forgot what it was like.

It had been Jake McCoy's idea to get Skinny

on the stage and into the way station as soon as they'd determined from the tracks they'd picked up that the girl and her rescuers were there.

Apart from getting a man on the inside who wouldn't be suspected, it also served the purpose of separating Skinny from Lefty. Jake had seen the pair of them whispering a few times and guessed they were planning something that wasn't exactly in his own best interest. As soon as this little business was over, he'd deal with the two of them— for now, it was a matter of keeping them apart and watching his back whenever they were around.

Aside from sending Skinny in on the coach, Jake intended to have Lopez ride in from the north a short time after the coach arrived. That would give him two men on the inside. When they were in place, he'd ride in with the rest of the bunch and take the girl back.

As for that damned Indian and the kid, he hoped they put up enough of a fight to get themselves killed. Everybody else would do well to keep their noses set to their own affairs and then they might not get hurt.

"There she sits!" called Jim Mitten from the box.

"What did he say?" asked the wine merchant.

"Comin' in to the way station," said the drummer, leaning his head out of the small window.

"Not before time," said the woman, brushing her hands down over the velvet skirt of her dress. She had surpisingly small hands, Skinny thought, watching them close. Fingers not much bigger than matchsticks that could be broke like a bird's leg.

He glanced at her face, the mouth a shade too small, cheeks flushed under the dust of the journey, eyes brown and wide and trying not to notice that they were being stared at.

Skinny shifted almost imperceptibly in the seat so that her side was pressed against his.

She noticed what he was doing and moved awkwardly away, pushing up to the side of the coach. Skinny laughed and winked his good eye. The woman shuddered and looked through the window. It was all that Skinny could do to keep his hand from repeating her own movement of moments before, smoothing down the rich velvet of her dress.

Jim Mitten shouted a greeting to the station as the coach swung round into the yard, Clem Watson standing out from the entrance to greet them, his hand raised in salute and a cheerful word on his lips. He'd known Jim for years and knew this to be his last trip. All he hoped was that the warning signs in his

bad leg had been wrong and that everything
was going to pass off peacefully.

As he led the team away a few minutes
later, Clem chanced to lift his head towards
the north and he picked out a solitary rider
heading down the trail towards the station.

Cuchillo was forking a mouthful of the thick
stew towards his mouth when the stage
slowed to a halt out front. He set the food
down again, untouched, his fingers instinctively travelling to his pistol and the haft of
the knife sheathed at his back.

There was no special reason to mistrust
any of the passengers arriving on the coach,
but right then especially Cuchillo was mis-
trustful of everyone. He'd got a good sight of
Jake McCoy back at the valley hideout, but
he wasn't certain if he could pick out any of
the others. Which meant that any man with a
gun at his belt was a potential enemy.

Marty had half-turned towards the door,
also, one hand resting gently on Natalie's
shoulder. The girl sat bent over her bowl of
scarcely touched food, not apparently noticing anything that was going on around her.

First through was the drummer, his leather
case of samples clutched in front of him with
both hands, the collar of his suit turned up

and the pants badly creased from the long journey.

He was followed by the wine merchant, tall and becoming fat at the belly, a dark mustache in need of trimming and his hair unruly and long. He wore a short-brimmed hat at an angle, gloves on his hands and an expression of superiority on his face.

The woman started to step through the door and hesitated as the thin man just behind her stretched forward his arm and held it back.

She murmured him a thank you which he hardly heard and carried on into the building. Skinny Ennis came through immediately behind her and by the time he was half way to the counter, he'd picked out the girl and the two who were with her.

Cuchillo looked at the lean gunman closely, but failed to pick him out.

Clem Watson was talking to the driver outside, the two of them taking the harness off the team that had ridden in and getting them into the corral. The passengers stood by the counter or sat down and waited. Cuchillo let them take a good look at him and then went back to his food, eating slowly and keeping his eyes skinned for the first sign of trouble, or of anyone taking more than a usual interest in the girl.

But no one did.

Clem came back inside with Jim Mitten and made a remark about a rider coming in from the north.

Cuchillo and Marty exchanged glances, neither one moving from his place.

Clem gave everyone a drink to break their thirst and clear the trail dust from their throats and then told the passengers that if they'd like to sit down, there was a plate of stew good and hot. He asked the woman if she'd like to wash up and she disappeared into the back room.

"Eat some more, Natalie," urged Marty softly, "you didn't ought to leave good stew like that."

"I don't want any more."

"You got to eat!"

Natalie shook her head and set her face away from the food, pushing her plate across the table.

"You listen to your brother now," said the whiskey drummer, who had taken a seat opposite. "You sure look as though you could build up your strength some."

"I tried to persuade her to take some of my patent medicine," put in Doc Murrayweather, "but she don't want that neither."

Cuchillo glanced round apprehensively as the sound of horse and rider came close to the station. If the station manager had been right, the man had come in from the north and there was no way McCoy should have been north of them, but a man could never be certain.

"You finished with this?" asked Clem, pointing down at Natalie's plate.

Natalie didn't answer; didn't seem to realize she was being spoken to.

"Sure, take it," said Marty with a helpless shrug.

Cuchillo held himself tense as the door opened and the Mexican came in. The Apache's pulse raced as he recognized the man for certain—or did he? The clothes, the wide-brimmed hat with the crown coming to a steep peak, the black leather gloves—all seemed identical. He looked at Marty and could see that the boy was doubtful, too.

Lopez played his hand well. He hardly looked around the room, made no eye contact whatsoever with Skinny, who was sitting eating at the far end of the table, across from an empty place where he hoped the woman passenger would sit.

The Mexican went to the counter and ordered a beer and a shot of tequilla and started talking to Clem about the hell of a ride he'd had down from Salinas.

Cuchillo caught Marty's eye and gestured

a question: the boy hesitated, glanced over his shoulder again, and signalled that he was uncertain.

Cuchillo ate the last mouthful of stew and broke off a chunk of cornbread and wiped it slowly round the inside of the plate.

The drummer and the wine merchant were talking business; Jim Mitten was leaning against the counter and eating his food there, putting in his couple of cents' worth every now and again along with Clem and the Mexican. Doc Murrayweather was hovering between table and counter, wondering who was the most likely to fall for his sales pitch. From his sonorous snores, it was clear that the prospector had fallen asleep in the heat from the stove.

Cuchillo gestured with one hand in Marty's direction, signalling that they should leave as soon as possible. Marty gave the girl a little shake and told her they were leaving.

His voice wasn't loud but it reached Skinny at the end of the table. The gunman slid his plate to the side and eased his body round so that he was facing more or less down the table.

If Cuchillo spotted the move then he gave no sign.

Marty stood up and put out a hand to help Natalie to her feet.

Cuchillo's fingers brushed the butt of his pistol as his hand moved to the table edge and he started to lever himself to his feet.

Skinny willed Lopez to turn around from his conversation and see what was going on.

Clem helped him out.

"You leavin' already?" he called across the room as Natalie stood rather shakily beside the table.

Then Lopez did turn and turned fast. His gloved hand ghosted to the butt of his gun and his free hand pushed him clear of the counter. At the end of the table, Skinny Ennis came up in a crouch.

Cuchillo picked out the Mexican and then the thin gunman a split second later. Right about one and fooled by the other. It wasn't going to matter.

"Get her down!" he called to Marty and ducked sideways between bench and table as the Mexican's pistol came up fast from its holster.

Cuchillo pulled his own gun from the waistband of his pants as he hit the floor. He used his elbows to propel his body under the table, moving fast and hoping to get a shot at Lopez as soon as he got his sights on him from the other side.

Marty struggled with the girl, finally swing-

ing her off her feet and down awkwardly to
the floor.

"Stay down where you are!" called Skinny. "Keep right there!"

Cuchillo angled himself forward another
six inches and snapped off a shot that sailed
well wide of the Mexican and broke three
bottles on the shelf back of the counter.

Lopez ducked and fired back, his bullet
screaming off the floor no more than six
inches away from the Apache's head.

Skinny Ennis took a couple of quick paces
sideways from the table end and as he did so
the door to the back room swung open behind
him.

Skinny's mind didn't think—it reacted automatically to danger.

He dropped low, swivelled, and shot the
woman from the stage coach through the right
breast.

Chapter Ten

She seemed to rock forward but that was in all probability an illusion. The certain reality was that when the back of her head struck the edge of the open door it sounded like an athlete striking a baseball for a home run.

Her mouth sagged open and her eyes dilated upwards; both her arms flapped outwards, striving for balance. A convulsive shudder ran up the length of her body and when it reached her head it wrenched her neck cruelly sideways.

Blood seeped through the front of her dress, deepening in color. She stumbled a few unco-ordinated paces towards the man who had seconds before fired a .45 slug through her body. The bullet had torn a hole the size of one of the woman's fists through the back of

her ribs and buried itself in the rear wall of
the back room.

Skinny Ennis stared at her, not able to take
in what had happened. There had been the
noise, someone threatening his back, he had
... he had ... he stared at the twisted face
as blood ran from the woman's nostrils and
from her ears. Sitting alongside her on the
stage she had been so warm, warmer than
any woman he had come close to in a long
time. And now ...

She lurched at the end of the table, eyes
closed and it was doubtful if she was feeling
even pain by now. Skinny took an instincitve
step back as she crashed down into the corner of the thick wood, driving plates to the
floor in a succession of smashes. Her hands
tried to grip and failed. She pitched from
sight beneath the table.

It had been a matter of seconds.

Marty had grabbed Natalie by the arms and
pulled her towards the front door. Cuchillo
watched Lopez duck down behind the counter, moved silently up behind Skinny Ennis.

The sound of galloping hoofs broke through
everyone's consciousness.

Marty left the girl and jumped to the window, staring out.

"McCoy!" he shouted.

Cuchillo hesitated a fraction too long, torn between dealing with the two men inside or making an escape while it was still possible.

Skinny rounded on him with the same speed as he had turned towards the back door, but this time his shot spun wide of Cuchillo's diving body. The Apache went forward with his left hand outstretched, the finger ends aiming for the gunman's throat.

As they succeeded in driving hard into Skinny Ennis' adam's apple, the gunman went down beneath the Indian's superior weight, pushing up with his knee as his back hit the floor. The knee caught Cuchillo inside the groin and made him wince with pain. As Skinny tried to kick himself clear, Cuchillo lashed out with his maimed hand, striking the man underneath the eye; with his other hand he freed the magnificent knife from its sheath.

Skinny Ennis glimpsed the lethal triangular blade and his eyes narrowed with something close to fear.

Marty leant his pistol against the bottom of the window and tried to knock a couple of McCoy's men out of the saddle. He chipped a piece of timber from the corral fence and came close to hitting one of the riderless horses in the leg, but otherwise achieved nothing.

The men dismounted and came at the place in a rush.

"Cuchillo!" Marty yelled, turning away from the window. "There's too many of 'em!"

Cuchillo was driving the knife at Skinny's chest and the sudden shout of his name made him steer his hand inches to the left of its target. Skinny called out as the side of the blade scored a line through the vest and shirt and the outer layer of skin, but did no more damage than that.

As Cuchillo drew back his knife arm, Skinny kneed him for a second time in the groin and followed up with a pistol-whipping to the head. The barrel cracked hard against Cuchillo's temple and the sight ripped a gash a couple of inches long above his eyebrow.

Marty scuttled across the room after the girl and had almost reached her when two men came through the front almost together. A few moments later another man ran through the rear and after that Jake McCoy strode through himself, not even bothering to draw either matching Colt from its holster.

"Ain't this real nice!" he announced sarcastically and reached, not for a gun, but for a short black cigar from his vest pocket. He fingered out a match and struck it against the sole of his boot, cupping his fingers around the cigar end until it had caught. Then he drew deep, slowly exhaled smoke through his nostrils, opened his mouth enough to let a smoke ring slide out and start its widening journey towards the low ceiling.

He surveyed the room. The two male passengers from the stage were still sitting close to the table, one of them with the remnants of a plate of stew smeared over his pants and coat. Jim Mitten and Clem Watson were up by the counter, both of them ready to take a hand if it became necessary, but calmed down by the fact that Lopez was crouching behind them, his pistol drawn and cocked.

Doc Murrayweather was standing a few feet away from the stove, fear writ large on his face and in his trembling hands.

The old prospector had woken up long enough to determine what was going on and now he sat low as he could in his chair, arms folded over his head and his eyes clenched tight shut.

Bitter moon kept guard alongside the rear door, looking now at the bleeding body of the almost-dead woman on the floor in front of him. Charlie Cloud was to McCoy's left, a Winchester in his hands, a shell ready in the chamber. Lefty Burnette was on McCoy's right side, looking questioningly at Skinny across the room.

Cuchillo leaned against the table, blood trickling down the side of his face from the blow he'd taken, his knife still in his hand but looking markedly less dangerous.

Marty crouched over the girl, who had gone down to her knees and whose mouth was working hard, chewing on something that was not there.

"Yeah," repeated Jake McCoy, "ain't this real nice!"

He moved a couple of paces deeper into the room and pointed down towards the woman's body. Blood was still dribbling from her nose and ear and her front was thick with it. "What the hell went down here?"

Skinny blinked his eye. "She . . . she come out that door behind me. I didn't know who she was."

McCoy laughed, a loud grating sound. "Just put one in her, huh? Always did say that bad eye of yours'd get you into a mess of trouble."

Skinny looked back at him with steady hatred and McCoy recognized it for what it was and laughed.

"Lopez!" he called across the room. "Bring me a bottle of whiskey out from there. Ridin' in like that made me dry as an old maid. . . ."

He broke off as he noticed Clem Watson

making a sideways move with his hand towards what might have been a stashed gun. Almost without effort, his right hand gun was out of its holster and levelled at the station manager, hammer thumbed back. "You weren't reckonin' on objectin' none, were you?"

Clem set a hand to the side of his face to still the tick that was beating away there. He shook his head and moved his hand back away from the shotgun. No bottle of whiskey was worth getting shot for—and if all they wanted was the girl, well, let them take her fast enough and let the rest of 'em alone.

"Go ahead," he said. "Go right ahead."

McCoy laughed: "Ain't that obligin'!"

Lopez threw him the bottle through the air. He could have caught it easily with his left hand, but doing the easy thing never interested Jake McCoy too much. Instead he waited until the bottle was sailing across the room, slid his Colt back into its holster and snatched at the bottle with the same right hand. Another laugh and he pulled the cork free with his teeth, spat it out, swallowed three times and belched loudly.

"Anyone else?"

Charlie Cloud grunted yes and McCoy turned the bottle over to him.

"Right! Now pry that kid away from our grub stake and we'll take the girl where no one ain't goin' to get her unless he's carryin' her daddy's money."

Bitter Moon started out from the back door, Lopez walked round the edge of the counter. Marty set himself in front of Natalie and spread his arms. His face was tight and beginning to sweat. His belly was hollow and his mouth was itching with dryness he knew came from fear. His pistol was angled into his belt and he figured he had maybe two slugs in the chamber. He flicked a glance across to Cuchillo, but the Apache was standing straight and tall and didn't seem about to get involved.

"Lefty," called McCoy, "you an' Charlie get out front and harness up a fresh team for that stage. We got to take this girl out of here, we might as well do it in style."

"The hell you will!" Jim Mitten pushed himself clear from the counter. He wasn't wearing a gun, but his temper was bristling and his fists were locked tight. He sure wasn't about to stand idly by and see his stage stolen from him in the middle of his last run. "That coach has got passengers an' mail to deliver and you ain't. . . ."

McCoy swaggered towards the driver and

jabbed a finger at his face. "Listen, old man. If you're good an' quiet we might let you walk away from this alive. You interfere an' the only way you'll get on that or any other stage again is in a cheap wooden box. You understand me?"

Jim Mitten looked at him. He understood.

"Lefty! Charlie! Get it done!"

The two men left the room and McCoy turned his attentions back to the girl. Bitter Moon and Lopez had made no further move towards Marty, who was still protecting her with outstretched arms. Over his shoulder, Natalie's face was white and blank.

"What the hell you waitin' for?" snarled McCoy. "If the kid don't get out the way, kill him."

Marty bit down on his bottom lip and thought about the two shells still in the chamber—he would never as much as get the pistol out from his belt.

"Marty!" Cuchillo's voice from the far side of the room was loud and deep.

"Injun! You keep out of this!"

Cuchillo ignored McCoy's words and continued to walk slowly around the table, passing the two terrified passengers and heading towards the door. "Marty," he said as he walked, "there is nothin' you can do here. Step away."

"What the hell d'you mean, step away? You think I'm goin' to let these murderin' bastards take her?"

Cuchillo looked at him evenly. "You cannot stop them."

"Hey, Injun!" shouted McCoy with a laugh. "You sure got it right." He laughed raucously again. "What is it they say? Somethin' 'bout talkin' with a straight tongue?"

A rattle of harness from beyond the door testified that the stage was being made ready. Jim Mitten chewed some on the inside of his mouth and nudged Clem Watson with his elbow. No one was paying the least attention to them now and Jim knew damn well the shotgun was only grabbing distance away.

Sweat dripped from the end of Clem's nose and his breathing got kind of noisy.

"How 'bout it, kid?" asked McCoy. "You goin' to listen to good advice or no?"

Marty slowly lowered his arms; he glanced over his shoulder and Natalie's eyes looked at him for a moment and then turned away. She was beginning to shake, almost imperceptibly, but Marty knew her well enough to be able to read the signs. He set his hands to her arms and held her to him, her hair against his mouth.

McCoy nodded an order to the two nearest men.

Lopez went up behind the boy and when he lifted his arms away, Marty scarcely resisted. Bitter Moon gave the girl a push from behind, urging her towards the door.

Cuchillo stood his ground, watching them move towards him. He was sure that getting Natalie outside was a good idea for her safety. If shooting broke out in that relatively confined space there was no telling who would get hit and how badly.

For an instant the girl hesitated before him and her eyes stared up into his swarthy face, but there was no expression to be read there. Bitter Moon set his hand against her back and propelled her past Cuchillo to the doorway.

"Stage's ready," announced Lefty, his head and shoulders appearing round the edge of the door.

"Get her inside and sit guard over her till I'm through here," said McCoy. "There's just one little matter needs settlin'."

Lefty took Natalie out to the waiting coach and helped her up the steps, the girl allowing him to guide her and offering no resistance. Bitter Moon and Lopez shifted a ways back into the main room. Like most of the others, they were looking at the big Apache, wondering what McCoy had in mind for him.

Cuchillo was wondering, too.

He was also wondering how long it was going to take the stage driver to pluck up sufficient nerve to drag whatever weapon was stashed under the counter out into the open. He knew that while everyone was interested in him, the driver was more likely to make his play—and he knew that it needed some diversion like that if he was going to get out of there in one piece.

"I don't care for girl," Cuchillo said flatly. "You do what you like with her."

Marty stared at him angrily, his head jutting forward at the Indian's words.

"What in the hell's name was you doin' up in the valley?" asked McCoy. "Didn't seem like you weren't interested in her then."

Cuchillo pointed at Marty. " He paid me. Now money gone. You do what you like."

McCoy laughed and Marty went at the Apache in a fury. He ran at him with his left fist clenched and his right hand grabbing at the pistol at his belt. McCoy let him get within four yards and then jutted out his foot and tripped the boy headlong. Marty went crashing down onto his left side, jarring his elbow and twisting his ankle beneath him.

Jake McCoy laughed and shook his head and Jim Mitten held his breath and grabbed

at the sawed-down stock of Clem's shotgun.
He was swinging it clear of the counter top
when Lopez saw the glint of the squat barrels and started to shout a warning.

McCoy arched round low, going for his
guns.

He was midway when Mitten loosed off
both barrels.

In a confined space that shotgun was capable of a whole lot of damage. Lopez had
had the presence of mind to yell a warning,
but not to move. He paid for that by taking
the most direct force of the blast, which lifted
him clear off his feet and deposited him like
a clumsy sack of potatoes against the front
wall. His front was torn open and lines like
the ragged scratches of a jealous whore bled
down both sides of his face. One eye was
closed and the other hung loose from its
bloody socket.

Doc Murrayweather had been turning away
and seeking the shelter of the stove when
some of the shot had laced down his back
and dug like fire into his neck.

On the ground and on his knees, Marty
had taken sufficient of the explosion to suf-
fer wounds to the shoulders and the top of
his back. Jake McCoy's left arm was torn
badly above and below the elbow; his Colt

slid slowly between his fingers, hit the floor
and skidded away.

"Kill the bastard! "McCoy shouted. "Kill
the old fool!"

He was looking over at Skinny Ennis, who
had an unimpeded view and whose gun was
already in his hand and pointing that way.

But Skinny had other ideas. He'd been
thinking about the perfect chance and he
figured that this was as close to being it as he
was ever going to find. He pivoted on his
right heel and fired twice. The first shot
smashed McCoy's left shoulder blade and
the second tore through his ribs and exited
with a welter of blood and fiber.

McCoy cursed and swayed back, clawing
for his other gun.

Back of him and to his right, Bitter Moon
brought up his pistol and shot Jim Mitten
through the throat. The stage driver rocked
back against the side of the counter, eyes
dimming fast. The sawed-off shotgun pitched
forward through his hands and he fell into
the arms of Clem Watson, dead.

"You treacherous bastard!" shrieked McCoy
and bit his lip with pain as he dragged his
body round and drew his other gun.

Bitter Moon fired again from the hip and
the bullet ricocheted off Skinny's hip bone
and then again off the rear wall.

As Skinny's legs slewed away under him Jake McCoy straightened his right arm and squeezed evenly back on the trigger of his Colt. A .45 slug punched into Skinny's heart and blasted a significant part of his left side all over the floor and the surrounding walls.

McCoy allowed himself a laugh and aimed the gun with care. He blew away the already dead man's one surviving eye before the pain got the better of him and he keeled over, falling to his hands and knees.

Marty lay on his chest, blinking between flashes of pain from his wounded back. He was looking for Cuchillo, but the Apache was nowhere to be seen.

As soon as Jim Mitten had opened up with the shotgun Cuchillo had seized his chance. Through the door with supple speed, he intercepted Charlie Cloud on his way across the yard. Cuchillo ducked underneath the swing of the Winchester and lunged forward with his left hand. The clenched fist itself would not have reached Charlie Cloud's body. The triangular blade gripped in it did. The razor-sharp point plunged deep into the Indian's belly and with a swift upward movement, Cuchillo opened him up like a pig on the slaughter block.

As Cuchillo pulled away, Charlie Cloud's

guts spilled out onto the floor of the yard, bloody coil by bloody coil.

"Jesus Christ!" hissed Lefty Burnette, mouth open, staring.

He stared too long.

Cuchillo had withdrawn the blade and now he lifted it fast over his shoulder. Lefty Burnette was standing up in the driver's seat, one hand holding fast to the roof rail, the other thinking to work his pistol. The great knife struck him low in the chest and buried itself almost to the hilt. Lefty's eyes opened wide and his arms flapped and flailed like a man drowning in midair. For several timeless moments he rocked back and forth along the seat before diving backwards and landing with a crunch on the back of his head alongside the front wheels.

Cuchillo jumped over the box after him, planting his disabled hand firmly on Lefty's breast and levering the blade back out, wiping the streaks of bright blood down the dead man's shirt.

Cuchillo slid the knife down into his sheath and drew his Colt. He peered through the windows of the coach at the way station door. From the sounds of shooting it seemed as if all hell had bust loose inside and he wondered for a few moments if anyone was coming out.

Then the breed jumped through the door, gun in hand, and Cuchillo fired three times, fast, but his aim with the Colt was not equal to that with the knife. Only one bullet hit Bitter Moon and that only gave him a flesh wound in the arm. Two of the breed's shots smashed high into the woodwork of the coach and Cuchillo ducked away from the window and jumped up towards the driver's seat. As he did so, Jake McCoy's gun pushed around the edge of the station window and fired a volley of shots at the coach. Bitter Moon dropped to one knee and started firing upwards. Wood splintered up around Cuchillo's face as he spotted the driver's sawed-off stashed down at the foot of the box. He dived for it and brought it up over the edge as a bullet streaked by his face so close he could feel the wind of its passing. Jake McCoy's face was clear at the window and Cuchillo didn't ask for anything more. He squeezed back on both triggers and the outlaw's face disappeared amidst a morass of splintered shards of bone and welts of flying blood and brain.

Cuchillo grunted in satisfaction as the face erupted and dropped the sawed-off back down. He rocked to his side and felt once more for the knife. He was about to hurl it through the air at Bitter Moon when Marty shot the breed through a slit in the door.

Inside the way station Clem Watson stood ruefully examining the carnage. The whiskey drummer shook and shivered and clung for support to his fellow passenger, who was sobbing uncontrollably through fear and relief that he was still alive and unharmed. Doc Murrayweather set his professional eye on the bodies and pronounced that none of them would any longer benefit from the powers of his famous cure-all and elixir.

"Wha?" mumbled the dazed old prospector. "Wha?"

Cuchillo dropped to the ground and pulled open the wrecked door of the coach, its woodwork torn and splintered with gunfire. He glanced quickly inside and turned as quickly away. Marty was coming slowly towards the coach, grimacing each time he set his foot to the ground.

"No." Cuchillo shook his head. "No."

Pain traversed the boy's face; pain more intense than anything caused by the wounds in his own back and shoulders. Somehow he got the energy to push his fists at Cuchillo and force him backwards. After several moments, the Apache shrugged and stood aside.

Natalie was curled across one of the seats as though sleeping, only she wasn't sleeping.

Which of the stray bullets had struck her was of no consequence now. Blood seeped through her clothing and collected in small, dark pools in its folds. Tiny speckles of it tinted her face with color for almost the first time. Her eyes were open and staring outwards, but they no longer seemed as wild and strange. Now there was something about them that told of peace and rest. Her hands were clasped together at her waist, almost in an act of prayer.

Marty stared down at her for a long time, oblivious to whatever else was going on around him. He failed to hear Cuchillo readying his mount, nor did he notice him climbing into the saddle.

Only when the pain from his wounds was nearing the unbearable, did the boy bend forward and touch his lips to the girl's mouth. It was cold as ice and when Marty's lips lifted clear they were smeared at one corner with a trace of blood.

Dimly, he walked back into the way station: dimly, he was aware of the sound of steady hoofbeats as Cuchillo rode away. Emptiness and waste tore at both their hearts— the white youth and the Apache. Marty's loss was still bleeding there in the way station yard, Cuchillo's bled in his memory and nothing except his own death would ever stem its flow.

The sky was beginning to darken to the southeast and the Apache rode towards it at a canter, grateful that he, at least, could ride away.

More bestselling western adventure from Pinnacle, America's #1 series publisher. Over 8 million copies of EDGE in print!

☐ 41-279-7 Loner #1		$1.75
☐ 41-868-X Ten Grand #2		$1.95
☐ 41-769-1 Apache Death #3		$1.95
☐ 41-282-7 Killer's Breed #4		$1.75
☐ 41-836-1 Blood on Silver #5		$1.95
☐ 41-770-5 Red River #6		$1.95
☐ 41-285-1 California Kill #7		$1.75
☐ 41-286-X Hell's Seven #8		$1.75
☐ 41-287-8 Bloody Summer #9		$1.75
☐ 41-771-3 Black Vengeance #10		$1.95
☐ 41-289-4 Sioux Uprising #11		$1.75
☐ 41-290-8 Death's Bounty #12		$1.75
☐ 40-462-X Hated #13		$1.50
☐ 41-772-1 Tiger's Gold #14		$1.95
☐ 41-293-2 Paradise Loses #15		$1.75
☐ 41-294-0 Final Shot #16		$1.75
☐ 41-838-8 Vengeance Valley #17		$1.95
☐ 41-773-X Ten Tombstones #18		$1.95
☐ 41-297-5 Ashes and Dust #19		$1.75
☐ 41-774-8 Sullivan's Law #20		$1.95
☐ 40-585-5 Rhapsody in Red #21		$1.50
☐ 40-487-5 Slaughter Road #22		$1.50

☐ 40-485-9 Echoes of War #23		$1.50
☐ 41-302-5 Slaughterday #24		$1.75
☐ 41-802-7 Violence Trail #25		$1.95
☐ 41-837-X Savage Dawn #26		$1.95
☐ 41-309-2 Death Drive #27		$1.75
☐ 41-204-X Eve of Evil #28		$1.50
☐ 41-775-6 The Living, The Dying,		
and The Dead #29		$1.95
☐ 41-312-2 Towering Nightmare #30		$1.75
☐ 41-313-0 Guilty Ones #31		$1.75
☐ 41-314-9 Frightened Gun #32		$1.75
☐ 41-315-7 Red Fury #33		$1.75
☐ 41-987-2 A Ride in the Sun #34		$1.95
☐ 41-776-4 Death Deal #35		$1.95
☐ 41-799-3 Town on Trial #36		$1.95
☐ 41-448-X Vengeance at		
Ventura #37		$1.75
☐ 41-449-8 Massacre Mission #38		$1.95
☐ 41-450-1 The Prisoners #39		$1.95
☐ 41-106-5 Two of a Kind		$1.75
☐ 41-894-9 Edge Meets Steele:		
Matching Pair		$2.25

Buy them at your local bookstore or use this handy coupon
Clip and mail this page with your order

PINNACLE BOOKS, INC.—Reader Service Dept.
1430 Broadway, New York, NY 10018

Please send me the book(s) I have checked above. I am enclosing $_____ (please add 75¢ to cover postage and handling). Send check or money order only—no cash or C.O.D.'s.

Mr./Mrs./Miss _____

Address _____

City _____ State/Zip_____

Please allow six weeks for delivery. Prices subject to change without notice.

George G. Gilman

ADAM STEELE

More bestselling
western adventure from Pinnacle,
America's # 1 series publisher!

☐ 40-378-X Death Trail # 12 $1.50
☐ 40-523-5 Bloody Border # 13 $1.50
☐ 40-524-3 Delta Duel # 14 $1.50
☐ 41-452-8 Tarnished Star #19 $1.75
☐ 41-453-6 Wanted for Murder #20 $1.95
☐ 41-454-4 Wagons East #21 $1.95
☐ 41-455-2 The Big Game #22 $1.95
☐ 41-914-7 Fort Despair #23 $1.95
☐ 41-894-9 Edge Meets Steele:
            Matching Pair $2.25
☐ 41-106-5 Two of a Kind $1.75

Buy them at your local bookstore or use this handy coupon
Clip and mail this page with your order

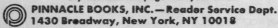 **PINNACLE BOOKS, INC. — Reader Service Dept.**
1430 Broadway, New York, NY 10018

Please send me the book(s) I have checked above. I am enclosing $_____ (please
add 75¢ to cover postage and handling). Send check or money order only—no cash or
C.O.D.'s.

Mr./Mrs./Miss _____

Address _____

City _____ State/Zip_____

Please allow six weeks for delivery. Prices subject to change without notice.

SIX-GUN SAMURAI

by Patrick Lee

FROM THE LAND OF THE SHOGUNS AND AMERICA'S #1 SERIES PUBLISHER, AN EXCITING NEW ACTION/ADVENTURE SERIES THAT COMBINES FAR-EASTERN TRADITION WITH HARDCORE WESTERN VIOLENCE!

Stranded in Japan, American-born Tom Fletcher becomes immersed in the ancient art of bushido—a violent code demanding bravery, honor and ultimate sacrifice—and returns to his homeland on a bloodsoaked trail of vengeance.

☐ 41-190-1	SIX-GUN SAMURAI #1	$1.95
☐ 41-191-X	SIX-GUN SAMURAI #2	$1.95
	Bushido Vengeance	
☐ 41-192-8	SIX-GUN SAMURAI #3	$1.95
	Gundown at Golden Gate	
☐ 41-416-1	SIX-GUN SAMURAI #4	$1.95
	Kamikaze Justice	
☐ 41-417-X	SIX-GUN SAMURAI #5	$1.95
	The Devil's Bowman	
☐ 41-418-8	SIX-GUN SAMURAI #6	$1.95
	Bushido Lawman	

Buy them at your local bookstore or use this handy coupon
Clip and mail this page with your order

Ⓟ **PINNACLE BOOKS, INC.**—Reader Service Dept.
1430 Broadway, New York, NY 10018

Please send me the book(s) I have checked above. I am enclosing $ _____ (please add 75¢ to cover postage and handling). Send check or money order only—no cash or C.O.D.'s.

Mr./Mrs./Miss _____

Address _____

City _____ State/Zip _____

Please allow six weeks for delivery. Prices subject to change without notice.

CELEBRATING 10 YEARS IN PRINT
AND OVER 22 MILLION COPIES SOLD!

☐ 41-756-X	Created, The Destroyer #1	$2.25
☐ 41-757-8	Death Check #2	$2.25
☐ 41-811-6	Chinese Puzzle #3	$2.25
☐ 41-758-6	Mafia Fix #4	$2.25
☐ 41-220-7	Dr. Quake #5	$1.95
☐ 41-221-5	Death Therapy #6	$1.95
☐ 41-222-3	Union Bust #7	$1.95
☐ 41-814-0	Summit Chase #8	$2.25
☐ 41-224-X	Murder's Shield #9	$1.95
☐ 41-225-8	Terror Squad #10	$1.95
☐ 41-856-6	Kill Or Cure #11	$2.25
☐ 41-227-4	Slave Safari #12	$1.95
☐ 41-228-2	Acid Rock #13	$1.95
☐ 41-229-0	Judgment Day #14	$1.95
☐ 41-768-3	Murder Ward #15	$2.25
☐ 41-231-2	Oil Slick #16	$1.95
☐ 41-232-0	Last War Dance #17	$1.95
☐ 40-894-3	Funny Money #18	$1.75
☐ 40-895-1	Holy Terror #19	$1.75
☐ 41-235-5	Assassins Play-Off #20	$1.95
☐ 41-236-3	Deadly Seeds #21	$1.95
☐ 40-898-6	Brain Drain #22	$1.75
☐ 41-884-1	Child's Play #23	$2.25
☐ 41-239-8	King's Curse #24	$1.95
☐ 40-901-X	Sweet Dreams #25	$1.75
☐ 40-902-8	In Enemy Hands #26	$1.75
☐ 41-242-8	Last Temple #27	$1.95
☐ 41-243-6	Ship of Death #28	$1.95
☐ 40-905-2	Final Death #29	$1.75
☐ 40-110-8	Mugger Blood #30	$1.50
☐ 40-907-9	Head Men #31	$1.75
☐ 40-908-7	Killer Chromosomes #32	$1.75
☐ 40-909-5	Voodoo Die #33	$1.75
☐ 41-249-5	Chained Reaction #34	$1.95
☐ 41-250-9	Last Call #35	$1.95
☐ 41-251-7	Power Play #36	$1.95
☐ 41-252-5	Bottom Line #37	$1.95
☐ 41-253-3	Bay City Blast #38	$1.95
☐ 41-254-1	Missing Link #39	$1.95
☐ 41-255-X	Dangerous Games #40	$1.95
☐ 41-766-7	Firing Line #41	$2.25
☐ 41-767-5	Timber Line #42	$2.25
☐ 41-909-0	Midnight Man #43	$2.25
☐ 40-718-1	Balance of Power #44	$1.95
☐ 40-719-X	Spoils of War #45	$1.95
☐ 40-720-3	Next of Kin #46	$1.95
☐ 41-557-5	Dying Space #47	$2.25
☐ 41-558-3	Profit Motive #48	$2.75
☐ 41-559-1	Skin Deep #49	$2.25

Buy them at your local bookstore or use this handy coupon
Clip and mail this page with your order

Ⓟ **PINNACLE BOOKS, INC.** — Reader Service Dept.
1430 Broadway, New York, NY 10018

Please send me the book(s) I have checked above. I am enclosing $_____ (please add 75¢ to cover postage and handling). Send check or money order only — no cash or C.O.D.'s.

Mr./Mrs./Miss_____

Address_____

City _____ State/Zip_____

Please allow six weeks for delivery. Prices subject to change without notice.